The Secrets of 24 Blackwell

Description:
The stories herein tend towards the su
goings on, time travel, witchcraft and other spooky -

They also touch upon social issues of the times they are set in, such as attitudes towards family values, same-sex love, relationships, religion, the class system and so on...

They will continue to flow from the author's imaginations and into print to become a series. The first compilation covers various periods in time up to and including the 19th century. Any subsequent books will deal with different timescales right up to the present day.

Intentions:
This series centres on attractive little building known as number 24 Blackwellgate, because we think it deserves to be famous simply for having managed to stay standing and intact for so long, whilst most of the other properties in the same street have been demolished and rebuilt in a different style all around it.

We also intend to expand our tales to take in Darlington in general, as we would love to clothe this beloved town in a mantle of legend, folklore, romance and mystery.

Whether part of the action takes place before number 24 was even built (as in Bridget's story), in the tunnels below it (as in Rachal's story), or in the rooms within it (as in Beryl's stories), this surviving architectural gem of Darlington is the original inspiration behind it all.

© 2016 and onwards infinitum

ISBN 978-1-326-77047-1

The Secrets of 24 Blackwellgate - Book One

The Secrets of 24 Blackwellgate - Book One

The Secrets of 24 Blackwellgate - Book One

They withdrew into the shadows and hatched their plots

Contents

LITTLE LAMB
Rachal 'Moonflower' Davidson

MERCY IN THE ATTIC
Beryl Maughan Hankin

DAMNED
Bridget Lowery

A GHOST AT THE DOOR: (Sarah's Story)
Beryl Maughan Hankin

THE HOMECOMING: (Simon's Story)
Beryl Maughan Hankin

The Secrets of 24 Blackwellgate - Book One

The stories in this book are fictional and are not intended to represent any actual events involving any person or persons living or dead.

The individual authors own the copyrights to their own stories in this book.
© 2016 and onwards infinitum
WARNING: The stories in this publication are not suitable for children as they contain some references to moderate sex and violence.

This book can be purchased from;
Guru Boutique, 24, Blackwellgate, Darlington or online from www.guruboutique.co.uk
Tel: 01325 461479
Also available from Lulu, Amazon, eBay and to order from most good bookshops.

Thanks go to Paul Magrs for providing us with our lovely front cover image, Jean Kirkup for inside illustration to 'Mercy In The Attic' and Jake Todhunter for design help.

Thanks also to Tracey Spark (on whom Beryl based her character Mrs Irene Sangster), Ray Hankin, Tony Smith, Colin Harrison, Kelly McWilliams, Emma Crawley, Andrew Finley, Tony Fox and John D Clare for advice and support.
The lady who supplied the Victorian items which inspired two of these stories and Beth, Amber and Courtney our lovely 'maids'.
Special mention has to be made of the staff at Crown Street Library, Darlington, for their invaluable help.

The Secrets of 24 Blackwellgate - Book One

Printed for Guru Boutique by Lulu
FOREWORD

Being first owner and then tenant of number 24 Blackwellgate, Darlington since 1990 has been a great privilege.
I love every stick, brick, stone and tile of the place.
I never feel so much at home as I do when I am there.
I am pretty certain my fellow workers in Guru feel the same, as it's so easy to soak up the history of the place.
When I look out from its upper arched windows with their pleasing shapes and adornments I can't help wonder about the people now gone who once inhabited the building and looked out from them before me.
Even on the ground floor, now perhaps a little different from how it must have been in the past, I feel a palpable sense of continuity.
I possibly love being in the basement the most, as there you cannot see that the outside world has changed around this little gem of a building as it still retains many original features (such as the imposing old fire range) and I feel transported to the past. The ground on which no 24 is built drops away sharply beneath it, so whilst the front part of the basement is underground, the back part isn't.
There is even a Secret Seven kind of tunnel leading out into Houndgate, at the back of the lowest level. Passing through it and unbolting three doors as I go, never fails to give me a little thrill of excitement.
I know that nothing lasts forever and that eventually I/we will have to leave this place and that makes me sad. I just hope that some part of my own and my fellow Gurus' souls will linger here long after we have gone.
Anyway, whatever the future holds, within the pages of this book some friends and I have tried to capture some of the magic and romance of our location, by linking it to stories,

which we have invented. These are tales from our own imaginations, inspired by the atmosphere of the building itself. It would be great to know what the real 'secrets' of 24 Blackwellgate are, as I am certain it has many from the past and perhaps even more yet to be revealed. After all, they do say 'truth is stranger than fiction'…
These old walls could surely tell many tales.
For now however, we (myself and these sympathetic friends of mine), have published herein a collection of our own unashamedly fantastical short stories etc., for all who wish to, to read them.
I hope you enjoy the fruits of our labours.
~Beryl. xx

The Secrets of 24 Blackwellgate - Book One

"On the 20th., January 2016 some friends got together in Voodoo Café, Darlington. They spoke about ghost stories and local history and each decided they had a tale to tell. This is mine."

Dedicated to my children xx
~Rachal

LITTLE LAMB

Rachal 'Moonflower' Davidson

'she faded from view and as if on a breeze, was carried back to that alleyway in Blackwellgate.'

The Secrets of 24 Blackwellgate - Book One

LITTLE LAMB

As he held his tiny newborn daughter in his arms he smiled. It had all been worth it, the move from Scotland away from his family and the long hours working for little money. He fell for Mary on a trip to Darlington. He had come to help his boss bring a herd of sheep to a local farm. The money was good and he enjoyed the travelling. Mary had been at the farm they delivered the sheep to and he had never looked back. He puffed out his chest and looked lovingly at his tired wife, 'she is the bonniest thing I have ever seen Mary. Thank you.' He leaned in and kissed her. He would make a wonderful life for his two precious girls.

BONNIE

Every step she took ended with her heel leaving her shoe. Stuffing the toes with rags didn't help them stay on and walking was hard and awkward. She pushed on determined to be at work on time. She loved her shoes. They were Mam's old shoes and too big but they were smart and had ribbons to tie them up. She liked her work and it was only twenty minutes away from home. She smiled, the quicker she started work the sooner she would be back home in front of the fire with a warm cup of tea. Da would be in bed and she would have the whole kitchen to herself. She neared The Fleece and clumped down the alleyway along the side of the pub and opened the back door. Greeted by the sound of laughter and blazing light she took a deep breath and started her night.

The evening went quickly enough, the usual round of jugs of ale, raucous laughter and the occasional hand on her bottom. She tried to ignore it, held her head high but gave no encouragement just like mam always told her. The evening was the same as all the others, the usual patrons, the same old stories and the endless serving of frothy jugs of beer. She called goodnight to the landlord and pulled on her coat. She buttoned it all the way up and held the collars close. She didn't like leaving the pub to walk home. Her dad used to meet her and they would sing songs and rhymes on the way back. One's that her mam had sung to them before she died. Dad didn't meet her now; he was sad and lonely and rarely left the house anymore. She steeled herself against the cold. The alleyway changed in the dead of night. The men from the fleece had bought their company and were mostly found to be up against the walls or being led by the hand into the building next door. Bonnie knew what went on in that place, she knew those ladies made their money by doing things with the men you should only do when you were married under God. It was none of her business, she had been brought up not to judge. She stepped quickly past the couples and kept her head down. As she neared the end of the alley she felt a hand on her head, her hair was grabbed and an arm snaked around her neck. A voice whispered vile words in her ear and she tried to break free from the vice she was in. The world went dark and a silent tear fell from her eye.........

DUNCAN
He couldn't hold back his tears as they lowered the coffin into the ground. His little lamb was gone forever and his heart was broken. First Mary, now Bonnie. He shouldered his heavy bag and left the graveyard, left Darlington and headed home to Scotland. Back to his roots and away from the pain that assaulted him here.

From behind the wall, she watched him leave and her heart broke too. She didn't want to let him go, how could she make him understand that she would love him forever. When she realised that she hadn't gone up to heaven she thought that maybe she was left here to watch over him but as she watched him leave she knew she had other work to do. She faded from view and as if on a breeze she was carried back to that alleyway on Blackwellgate.

Since the night she died she had explored the buildings and had found some amazing places. Bonnie wondered if anyone knew about the tunnels. They were so dark and warm. They led from the churchyard under the town in many directions. One led straight under 24 Blackwellgate, the brothel near to The Fleece. It was dirty and dripped water but muffled the sounds from the street above and it felt like home. Although she didn't need to sleep or eat she felt safe and secure there.

She sometimes liked to sit in The Fleece, watching her old customers and her old boss. It felt strange to watch them all and be invisible to them. She giggled at their jokes and bad words and felt sad that she wouldn't ever join in with the fun again. She especially liked to watch David, he was her Dad's dearest friend and he looked so sad since Dad had left Darlington to go home. David had been like family to them all after mam had died.

Bonnie wondered if Mam was really in heaven or here somewhere still.

DAVID

One warm evening as the last of the men had staggered from the pub, Bonnie followed them out into the alley. She wanted to go back to her tunnel. Ahead of her she saw a young girl, walking, almost running towards the street. A man stepped in front of Bonnie, his back to her as he quickly marched towards the scurrying girl. Bonnie felt alarmed, she didn't want to see what happened but was powerless to do anything as he caught up with the girl and snaked his arm around her neck. He moved quickly and pulled the girl into a side door that led down to the basement of the brothel. Bonnie followed.

The man kept a tight grip on the whimpering girl and opened a hatch in the floor with his free hand. It revealed another way into the secret tunnels. He pushed the girl into the darkness and jumped down after her, pulling the hatch closed behind him.

Bonnie knew what was happening and was so scared. She couldn't help, but she couldn't leave the poor girl alone. With a blink, she was down in the tunnel with them and saw as the man straddled the young girl, his hands on her neck. He was saying cruel and vile things to her and Bonnie felt cold. She knew who this was. She knew now who had hurt her. Silent tears fells from her cold face. Not tears of sadness, she was angrier than she had ever thought possible. David was straddling that poor innocent girl. David the man who had been almost part of her family, like an uncle.

A strong wind blew through the tunnel, David stopped for a moment, wondering where that draught had even come from. He grabbed the girl again and suddenly felt himself lifted and thrown against the tunnel wall. He couldn't see anyone, yet he could hear the wind now howling and mingling with the cries of his latest victim. He tried to stand and managed to get to his knees. In front of him, the air shimmered and brightened and before him stood another young girl. It was impossible. Bonnie! Bonnie was in front of him still dressed in the coat and shoes she wore when he had killed the brazen little thing. He tried to rise to his feet and get away but she was gaining strength and as the wind tore through the tunnel she reached for him, the tunnel shone with light and Bonnie grabbed his hands.
Bonnie knew what she had to do. The light grew and the wind howled and she held fast to David's hands. She could leave now. She could step into the light and take him with her. No more

killing for David, no more pain for anyone. With every bit of strength she had, she pulled David with her as she stepped into the wind and then into the light.

The End

The young girl dared to peek up around the tunnel.
The man was gone. The wind was gone. At the far end of the tunnel, she could see some rough steps carved into the wall. She ran and leapt up the steps. She reached a door that led into the back room of the Fleece. She paused for breath and then screamed. They came running, the landlord, and his wife. The girl was never able to tell them what really happened but she knew she had been saved and who had saved her.
'Thank you Bonnie,' she whispered.

The Secrets of 24 Blackwellgate - Book One

GOODBYE BONNIE

To walk the town in darkness,
into the tunnels deep
To hear each sound and secret
and know when you all weep
To slip through walls and windows
and watch you when you're asleep
To hold your hand and kiss you,
your secrets I can keep

I think my job is clear now;
I'm keeper of the night
I am here to save you all,
the one that has to fight
I'm not sure I am strong enough
but try with all my might
To lead you all and guide you upwards
into the light

I don't think I was ever meant to feel this hate
I don't believe in those who tell me all of life is fate
I don't think I can suffer this
I don't think it's too late
I don't want to be forever here beneath Blackwellgate

The Secrets of 24 Blackwellgate - Book One

'This story is dedicated to all those who belong to Guru Tribe, whoever and wherever they may be'
~Beryl

MERCY IN THE ATTIC

Beryl Maughan Hankin

'All they had was each other and little Mercy was their focal point'

The Secrets of 24 Blackwellgate - Book One

The Secrets of 24 Blackwellgate - Book One

MERCY IN THE ATTIC

Those present when Mercy was born would never forget what happened up there in the attic of 24 Blackwellgate that night. Even the heavens seemed angry.
Torrential rain lashed down, sheet lightening lit up the sky, soon to be followed by deafening thunder, which shook the very foundations of the house where they were all imprisoned. The storm raging outside was a fitting accompaniment to the human drama playing out within that tragic space.

Maria was the name of the pretty young girl lying on the bed and she worked as a prostitute. She was in an advanced state of pregnancy but had hidden this fact from the brothel owner. It was only when she removed all her clothing that anyone could tell, and that very night a brutish client when he realised her condition had felt cheated and decided to punish her for it. The attack had now brought on the birth of her baby before it was due. She was in a great deal of pain, but still mustered up the strength to defiantly curse all those who had mistreated her. She cursed her drunken mother, she cursed the man who had hurt her tonight and most of all she cursed Ezra Hardesty the owner of this hellish place for making profit from the misery of others.
The contractions were becoming ever more frequent. Her friend Maureen stroked her brow with a cool damp cloth and tried to sooth her. The others stood around wanting to help, but not knowing what they could do. She hardly knew they were there as she was delirious and her mind was experiencing vivid flashbacks to the past.
When as a child she had been sold to Ezra to work in his whorehouse, by her own gin soaked mother, Maria had promised herself that one day she would escape this degrading way of life. She dreamed she would meet a good man, get wed,

have a family of her own and care for those babes in the way she wished she had been cared for herself. She was an intelligent, courageous girl and once she had been at the brothel long enough to experience what went on, she rebelled. Passionately convinced that it was wrong that one human being could have such absolute power over the fate and well being of another, she complained to Ezra about the way she and her fellow inmates were constantly allowed to be so badly abused by their clients. She had bravely stood up to Ezra saying that she hated the work, which had become her lot, but if it had to be done she and the other girls deserved to be better protected.

She remembered the savage beating he gave her for her trouble, as he wanted to make an example of her to show the others what happened if they made trouble. From that day onward she had vowed she would make him pay for his cruelty. How she could keep that vow now she did not know, as she was conscious enough to realise not only was she about to give birth, but also seriously injured to such a degree that she may not survive.

The father of Maria's imminent child was not of course the good husband she had yearned for to save her from her miserable situation. This baby would had been conceived during a coupling with some stranger, who had given Ezra a few coins for the use of her body and then would have most probably forgotten all about her once he had left the premises. For her own part she didn't even know which of the many men she had lain with was responsible for her condition.

She had realised that in her circumstances she should have asked Ezra to arrange an abortion, but she hadn't been able to bring herself to be party to such a thing, as the life she carried inside her seemed significant in some way and had given her hope.

Now she was paying the ultimate price for that decision, as she was most likely dying due to the actions of a more recent and more violent nameless paying customer.
Then all those thoughts vanished as the birth became imminent...
Maria emitted a soul-piercing scream as the child was ejected from her body in one final blood drenched push and her spirit was liberated from its human bonds in that same moment. She had battled with death and lost, but part of her would live on in this baby.
As the mother took her last breath, her daughter gasped her first.

Against all the odds the infant had survived.

Maria's friends named the baby Mercy, because that was what they had shown to her in the early hours of that terrifying Friday morning when she was first thrust into this world.
To conceal the sound of the child's early cries they made certain the door to the room she occupied was tightly closed at all times and hung heavy drapes over it to muffle the sound even more.

Mercy was now six years old, and she knew she must stay the attic. They told her it was for her own safety and she never questioned that.
She knew she had been born into the world on the narrow bed she was sitting cross-legged on now, having been told this fact by the people she lived amongst.
She knew she must wash and dress every morning.
She knew she must keep very quiet and hide under the bed if she heard anyone coming up the stairs.
Apart from those things she didn't know very much else as she had never had the chance to learn.

There were three rooms in her attic world and Mercy knew every inch of them all.
The five older girls in the house slept up here also. They usually took their rest during the daytime, unless they were ill or had been hurt, as they were always up and working on the next floor down from late in the evening until well into the early hours.
Whilst the girls were thus engaged she was left on her own for long periods of time and used to listen for noises coming from downstairs. Mostly it was the sound of forced laughter or chatter, but sometimes raised voices, slaps and screams were also heard in this house late at night. When that happened she felt sad, as she knew that something bad must be happening to one of her friends and she would start to sob. On those occasions a benign presence seemed to join her on the bed and she would sense an invisible hand stroking her hair and that always comforted her and calmed her down.
She wasn't afraid as she knew that whatever was there would not harm her and meant her well.
She never spoke to her friends of this, as she was afraid that if she did the comfort would stop and she didn't want that to happen.

She and the other females who inhabited these premises had become as near to being a family as people in their situation could get.
All they had was each other, and little Mercy was their focal point.
Since the day she was born her protectors had always brought her a share of the milk, and later food as well, supplied to them daily by their owner. During the day when no one else was in the house and they had time on their hands, they would talk to her, tease her, chase her, cuddle her, tickle her and make her laugh.

She was their little pet.

There was a front window in the attic.
Mercy loved to peep through the lace curtain and look down from the window at those in the street below who must be more fortunate than she was, as they seemed to be able to come and go as they pleased.
There were so many wonderful sights to see out there.
From listening to the other girls she learnt the names of some of the things she could see from the window and a little about what those other people did, such as the fact that some of them rode around in carriages pulled by creatures called horses.
She learnt only what was directly relevant to her own limited existence but it was enough for now. The main thing was that she was here at all.
None of the girls in the house could read or write, but that didn't concern Mercy, as she didn't know what reading or writing was.
She did know however that they cared about her and she loved them back.
She liked them to tell her about the things they did when they were away from her.
To make her laugh they often described some of the antics the callers who came to the house late in the evenings got up to.
They had special names for many of them, especially the regulars.
Mr Jelly-Belly and Mr Wobbly-Bot were just two of the names that always made her squeal with amusement.

The others knew that they themselves all belonged to Ezra, the owner of the property.
Ezra visited the house at least twice a day.

He came every morning to bring provisions and check on domestic things and every night to oversee the running of his business.

This was why Mercy had been trained to stay out of the way, as they never knew when he was due.

Sometimes he would bring a workman with him to mend something, but he wasn't concerned about the state of the attic and never arranged for any work to be done up there.

Other times a woman was brought in when a girl had 'fallen wrong', and whatever she did to abort the foetus was done in a room on the ground floor, in private.

So far, none of these people had ever had cause to visit the very top of the house, so the secret the girls shared had up to now been safe.

In the evenings, Ezra stayed downstairs near the door. First, he always checked that the females in the line up were presentable, then would proceed to take the money from the gentlemen callers.

One by one these men arrived, chose a partner and disappeared upstairs.

Whilst this was going on he liked to semi-doze in his big comfortable chair, and only woke to let people in or out and finally to close the premises up, locking the girls inside for the night.

Due to his arthritic hips, Ezra even found it difficult to climb the stairs to the first floor so he avoided altogether having to venture as far as the attic.

He hadn't been up there for as long as anyone could remember.

He just instructed the girls to keep themselves and their beds clean and the rooms swept and dusted.

They seemed quite capable of doing that so he was content to let them get on with it.

His head girl was Maureen, the tall red haired Irish lassie. She didn't say much, but she was bright enough for his purposes and could count. Several times a week she would let him know what household supplies were required and inform him of any other matters needing attention.

He would even allow her to accompany him into the outside world when he wanted her to help him with some errand or other.

She never told him that six years ago a baby had been born on the very top floor, or that she and the other girls fearing for its safety and out of loyalty to its mother, had decided to hide the child and care for it themselves.

All he did know was that six years back Maria, one of his more troublesome 'investments', as he called the young women he had imprisoned in this house of ill repute, had been reported dead.

The stupid wretch was pregnant at the time but had not told him.

If he had been informed he would have asked the woman who dealt with these situations for him, to come to the house and sort it out.

As it was the girl died from blood loss following a blow to the stomach from a disgruntled client during one of her nightly encounters.

Ezra assumed the child had still been inside her and so was also dead.

He'd arranged for her body to be disposed of privately and thought that was the end of the matter.

The other girls had deeply mourned the passing of one of their number, but on the day that she was taken away they seemed curiously excited, which puzzled him.

Little did he know it was because they had a secret, which was hidden away in the attic.

He decided their mood was because they accepted life must go on and were glad it wasn't them who had passed away and that pleased him. The last thing he wanted was to see miserable faces greeting his callers so just to make doubly sure they were in good fettle for the work that lay ahead of them that night, he brought them in a jug of gin to share between them.
After finishing the gin off, the girls, now in a tipsy state, decided that although Ezra was indeed a nasty piece of work, they could have had an even worse master, as at least they always had enough to eat and he himself never troubled them in the manner the other men did.
They also agreed that he didn't like it when customers hit any of them too hard or hurt them in other ways, but guessed that was only because it may prevent them from working for a few days. Then they remembered what happened to poor Maria and that sobered them up and they went back to fearing and disliking him intensely.
These girls weren't stupid they were just poor and uneducated.

One day Mercy said to one of her best friends, "Elsie, where did I come from?"
Elsie told her, "You came from your mam, and then she died." Mercy didn't know what she meant so asked, "Why did she die?" "I think it was because she didn't ask Ezra to get Mrs Dunne to take you out of her tummy," said Elsie.
Mercy thought about that for a long, long time.

During the daytime, in their own ways the child and her adoptive young 'mams', were as happy as people in their situation could be, even though they were always on their guard in case Ezra turned up unexpectedly.

Apart from that worry, once they had done their cleaning duties their time was their own for a few hours and they could rest.

It was the nights they dreaded, as they never knew what was going to happen.

One night a drunken man who on his way out was supposed to have gone downstairs, had taken it into his head to go upwards instead and had stumbled into the attic.

His eyes alighted on Mercy. She had never seen a man up close before and shouted to Elsie for help.

Elsie, who had just said goodbye to her final visitor of the night heard the child calling her name and knowing this was unusual, rushed to her aid.

She led the man back down to the ground floor but couldn't prevent him from telling Ezra what he had seen.

"Bring her to me," Ezra ordered.

Elsie refused so he struck her.

The next girl he asked refused as well.

Just as he was about to strike her too, the child appeared. She was confused as she had never been out of the attic before, but now that the secret was out there seemed no point in staying there as it would only cause trouble for her friends.

Ezra's eyes lit up when he saw her.

"You're coming with me," he announced grabbing her arm, "I know exactly what to do with you."

The girls all gasped in horror, as they could not allow this to happen to their 'baby'.

They wondered what he wanted with her. He might intend to kill her. He couldn't. She was theirs.

Apart from the girls themselves the child and Ezra, there was no other living soul around as all the men had gone now.

They should have tried to stop him then and there, but they were so used to doing as they were told and it had all happened so quickly that they didn't. Instead they were all frozen to the spots where they stood.

In stunned silence, they watched him drag their 'baby' towards the front door, and then both were gone and they heard the old man lock the door behind him.

Maureen suddenly said, "I know where he lives, he once took me there to pick up some fresh bed linen."

Without even speaking, they all knew what they had to do. The problem was how could they get out of the house as the door was locked, and all the windows, apart from the attic ones which were too high to escape from anyway, had sturdy shutters which were also securely locked.

Normally they never went into the basement as they had been warned that the stairs were rotting away and it was dark, dusty and half full of rubbish.

Ezra said there were rats and huge spiders down there too, so they had tried to forget it even existed.

However, they were desperate so this time they decided to investigate hoping there may be a long forgotten way out.

Maureen pushed open the door to see what was beyond it. Just as Ezra had said there was a flight of dangerously damaged wooden steps leading into pitch-blackness, and the way down was swathed in cobwebs. Elsie brought a candle and the determined girls nervously followed her as she led the way. They stumbled over big dead fly bloated rats, planks of timber and bricks and rubbish of all kinds and were just about to give up when in the flickering light of the candle they saw a door. The bolts in this door were rusted closed and had obviously never been opened for years. At first they thought they could never hope to move them. Then as Maureen was taking her turn at trying to open them, they heard a grating sound and the biggest bolt, which was in the middle started to shift. That

gave them renewed strength and finally they succeeded to slide it open. Then they did the same with the top bolt, and soon managed to free the bottom one too.
At the other side of the door was a vaulted passageway that led out onto a street. They were free.
It had taken them a considerable length of time to open those bolts and they worried that they would be too late to help their much-loved child.

Maureen found the way to Ezra's house, which was in a lonely part of a long road down by the river Skerne.
Now they had to decide what to do next.
They were very afraid.
They entered his garden and huddled at the side of the building, hidden from view in the dark amongst the bushes.
They were all wondering what was happening to Mercy.
The house had a stable attached to it, and the next thing that occurred was that Ezra emerged from that stable holding onto the reigns of a tired looking horse.
He then hitched the horse to a small trap.
When he reached his front gate he tied the horse to a post, which had been sited there for the purpose and went back up the path to his home. Soon he returned dragging a lumpy looking hessian sack behind him. The neck of the sack was tied tightly with string. The girls guessed what was in that sack and feared the worst. They watched as the old man struggled to heave it onto the vehicle, and they thought that once it was on board he would get into the driver's seat beside it and drive off and they realised that if they were to stop him, it was now or never.
But no, he turned back to lock his door.
That was the signal they needed. Just as he was withdrawing the key, like a pack of banshees, they charged at their master

throwing stones they had collected for the purpose and waving sticks and branches they had picked up in the bushes.

He couldn't get back into the house because the door was now locked. He fumbled to put his key back into the keyhole to unlock it, but his fingers were crippled with arthritis and just would not turn it quickly enough.

The women were almost upon him now, so he abandoned the attempt to open his door and hobbled off across the road as fast as he could, to try and escape them.

A bright light, which the girls thought may have been a reflection from the moon, seemed to be following just behind him.

Across the road was the river Skerne, and in his haste to get away Ezra, now enveloped by the strange light seemed to lose his footing on the slippery grass bank and fall into that river, headfirst.

The angry pack following him saw him fall.

He must have hit his head on a rock or something as he went in because he didn't struggle to get out of the water, which now covered the upper part of his body.

He just lay; face down where he had fallen, totally still and partly submerged in the muddy Skerne.

It was as if some unseen force held him there…

The girls' first instincts were to try and get him out.

Then they remembered the sack, which they were certain contained Mercy.

They didn't even know if she was dead or alive, so they crossed back over the road to find out.

When they got there the horse was straining at his tether but was unable to break free. Maureen went to his head to calm him and the others leant into the trap to try and open the sack. They untied the knots and pulled the hessian back and to

their great joy found that their little one, although bound at her hands and feet, and gagged with a dirty rag, was alive. Once she was free Mercy clung to Elsie as if she would never let go again, and all the girls tried to kiss her tears away. She was very upset but seemed quite unharmed. Between sobs she revealed to them that Ezra had told her he was going to sell her to a "mucky man," who would pay him a lot of money for the pleasure of owning a little girl. She had cried out and tried to kick him when he told her that, which is why he had tied her up and put her in the sack to keep her quiet.
They now turned their attention back to Ezra.
The strange light, which had flickered near him had gone, but he was still lying motionless across the way, partly submerged under water.
Given the time that had passed without him stirring that could mean only one thing. He had drowned.
Now they all felt fearful.
What was to happen to them? How would they eat? Where would they live? They had nothing of their own. They might be blamed for his death.
What were they to do?
Then the plumpest one of them all, Nancy, pointed out that the key was still sticking out of the lock in Ezra's front door.

The next morning when the body of a man drowned in the river was reported to the authorities, there was an investigation.
It looked very likely that the deceased had been intending to go somewhere with his horse and trap but had probably decided to take a piss in the river first and fallen in.
His home nearby was securely locked up.
The key to it was in his pocket.
Foul play was not suspected.

On further inspection, although there seemed to be nothing of real value inside his dwelling, there was no sign that anything had been disturbed either.
Everyone knew he had connections with the local brothel, so enquiries had to be made there to try and find out what the state of the man's health had been when last seen.

At first, when the policemen arrived at the whorehouse in Blackwellgate they couldn't get in.
The front door was secured on the outside as if it were a prison and the women on the inside had no means of opening it either, so they had to send someone back to the dead man's house to find a key.
They felt a tad sorry for the women who were trapped like that, so obviously unable to leave the premises unless someone came to let them out.
It never crossed anyone official's mind to suspect that down in the filthy rubble filled cellar there was a hidden way out and as long as the bolts were left open, which they had been last night, back in again.

When eventually the key to the main door was brought and the officers of the law managed to get in to ask their questions, they saw that the females inside seemed genuinely shaken up.
It was assumed that they were upset by the news of their master's death and the realisation that with him gone they would now be rendered homeless.
Sad though that was, it was no concern of those involved in tidying up the formalities surrounding Mr Hardesty's death.
They quietened any twinge of conscience they may have had by agreeing between themselves that very likely some poorhouse would take these women in.
What the policemen didn't know was that the real reason for the girls' subdued demeanour had little to do with any of that,

but a lot to do with still being in shock from something that had happened when they got back from their rescue mission last night.

On returning to the 'prison', which was their only home, they had carefully slid the bolts back into place behind them and made sure plenty of rubbish was blocking the door they had just returned through.
They made their way out of the basement and then up two more sets of stairs to the top of the house to put Mercy to bed, as the poor mite was exhausted.
As the child slept oblivious to it all, something almost unbelievable started to happen before the eyes of the other five girls.
First of all the rain began. It was just a shower at first but it got heavier and heavier. A howling wind got up.
Before long the rain was lashing on the windowpanes. Then the lightening flashed and the thunder rumbled and they were reminded of that fateful night when they had lost one friend and gained another. A brilliant flash of sheet lightening suddenly illuminated the dimly lit room, and in that dazzling few seconds they could just make out in the midst of it, the hazy flickering image of their dead friend framed by a halo of even brighter light. She looked calm and beautiful and told them not to be afraid, but of course they were afraid, as they all suddenly realised that this was the same spirit, which had made sure that Ezra drowned in the river last night.
The girls huddled together nervously as Maria's ghost, as that was what they had decided this must be, lay down beside the sleeping form of her child, on that same birthing bed where she had lost her life.
She lovingly stroked the sleeping Mercy's hair and whispered the words, "We have won. We are free. Where you go, there be me."

Then as quickly as she had appeared she vanished again and all that remained was the sound of her laughter; soft at first but building up until at its loudest it was echoing around the attic walls, filling the whole space until it reached a glorious triumphant crescendo. Eventually the sound dropped and grew fainter and fainter until it was barely audible at all and then it stopped.
The noise of the storm outside had also waned and things once again returned to what seemed to be normal.
Had Maria's spirit really gone or was she still here guarding her offspring but invisible to their eyes and undetectable to their touch? These were questions to which only time would provide the answers but for now all this band of friends wanted to do was sleep.

After the visit from the police on the morning after the drowning, a few days passed with no further word from anyone and everyone in the house just waited to see what would happen next.
Then word came that the dead man's next of kin had been informed of the situation and the formalities concerning his death had been completed.
The property was now going to be stripped of all but the basics and a full inventory taken.
The girls were asked to stay on for a while to clean the place up.
Once they had done that they were told to vacate the premises in order for it to be put up for sale. As payment for their efforts they were given a few shillings and allowed to take a wheelbarrow with them to carry away some food and their few personal possessions when they left.
As the six girls filed out it was noted that one of them was a mere child. The red-haired lass lifted the little girl up and sat

her on top of the barrow, and then they all trudged off down the road.
Where they were going no one really cared...

Several days later Maureen, Elsie, Nancy, Sally, Joan and Mercy were far enough away from Darlington to start to take in the fact that they each had more gold coins than they had ever seen in their lives. Each of the girls had hidden her share of the coins in her undergarments in order to smuggle the gold out. Now that the danger of being discovered was over Maureen remarked, "that's the best thing that ever got in to our bloomers ladies." This sent the girls in to fits of relieved laughter causing tears of mirth to roll down their faces. On a more serious note they knew that now they all had a future and it was up to them what they did with it.
They knew that they, and those that had gone before them, often painfully and sometimes fatally as in Maria's case, had earned that gold which they had taken from the whoremaster's home on the night that evil man had died.
Because of this, they felt that they had done nothing wrong at all.

Number 24 Blackwellgate soon had new and respectable owners, who updated the whole place, and installed a flight of stone steps and a large expensive fire range in the basement. The building changed hands several times after that, and memories of what the premises had formerly been used for gradually faded away with time.

Every once in a while, right down to the present day, people sometimes swear they hear the sound of triumphant laughter ringing out in the attic.

The Secrets of 24 Blackwellgate - Book One

"We have won. We are free.
Where you go, there be me"

The Secrets of 24 Blackwellgate - Book One

DEDICATION

"Without the unique history of Darlington there would be no story.
Without Crown Street Library my work would be less well informed.
Without my family I would not write.
My story is dedicated to Robbie and Robert."
~Bridget

DAMNED

Bridget Lowery

"So, alone she sat, alone she cried, alone she prayed."

Author notes:

- Betsy, a character in my story, **Damned**, lives in 24 Blackwellgate. In the 1600s the building did not exist as it is in its present state but research tells me that in early 1600s there were, "5 houses of prostitution in Blackwellgate". It is likely that one of these was the beginnings of number 24.

- To avoid confusion the streets are named using their modern form, for example Blackwellgate was originally called Bathel Gate or Gata (Gata: from the Danish for Street).

BL

The Secrets of 24 Blackwellgate - Book One

DAMNED

In Cromwell's England you do not want to be labelled as a witch, a Catholic, or a Royalist – in fact, it is safer to be as invisible as possible. Living in 1650s Puritan England has its drawbacks; that is not to say there are no positives to the New Order. It brings with it exactly what it preaches, Order. People know what they can and cannot do; there is a disciplined, loyal army and generally speaking there is peace in the land, mainly because everyone is terrified of upsetting the Lord Protector (Oliver to his friends) and his Major Generals.

Jane Atkinson lived to rue the day she upset the local Major General, Edward Linton.

ONE

Jane had a very happy childhood; she ran and sang and played in the fields surrounding her home. She even learned to read and write at the local school for children of the poor. The Catholic-hating Cromwell had not yet surfaced so she was free to follow her mother to Church, to say her prayers and to fear the Devil.

Whether Puritan or Catholic, *all* should fear the Devil. He gets everywhere. He can squirrel into your brain and turn your thoughts to evil doings; he is there, alongside God, for every decision you make. His is the path of least resistance; but sometimes it's the only path ... a path that can damn you to hell.

Jane was young when she started work as a maid in the Bishop of Durham's Palace in Darlington. Her first job of every day was to lay the fires. It was a big house with a fire in every room and as Jane carried buckets full of coal into room after room her young muscles ached. The work was tedious as well as back-breaking and was followed by a round of general duties around the house and sometimes, if she was lucky, shopping at the market.

The Palace was kept by Bishop Grace as a place for visiting dignitaries to stay. One such visitor was Edward Linton. He brought with him his wife and extensive entourage. As one of Oliver Cromwell's Major Generals, tasked with controlling the hotbed of Darlington and environs, Edward Linton needed a base. He had had his eye on the Bishop's Castle at nearby Auckland, but strategically, Cromwell required him to be more central and able to provide shelter and provisions for an army if need be. Darlington served his purposes. Bishop Grace made Edward very welcome at his residence within the town, lying just south of the town Church and therefore quite central. He told Edward he should exercise free reign as lord and master of the Palace for as long as he needed to stay.

During Edward's first few months he had not noticed Jane. Recruiting men, planning campaigns, banqueting, carousing ... it all took effort and, as a Puritan, he also had to genuinely tussle with his conscience every time he went with that pretty little prostitute in Blackwellgate. The Bishop had recommended Betsy, so her reference was unquestionable. She was housed far enough away from Edward's residence to allow him to believe his wife would never meet her, and of course she had been threatened with swift death if she ever spoke of him. Under cover of dark he would make his way up Tubwell Row, cross the market place onto High Row and then cross to the corner of Blackwellgate. It was a circuitous route that was designed to be his evening walk and to fool the locals into thinking he was exercising. He counted the doors to number 24, where he always received a warm welcome. He made his exit from the rear of the building onto Houndgate and from there he walked over the open ground to his home, to lie in the arms of his unsuspecting wife. He always slept well.

Betsy made Edward very happy. Her angelic beauty and curvaceous body attracted him and she knew not to chatter and annoy him. He paid her well enough, she performed nicely and for the present all was well.

If only Edward had been satisfied with two women.

TWO

Inevitably, the day dawned when Jane's path crossed Edward's. It was a beautifully sunny morning and Jane enjoyed feeling the warmth of the sun as she hung out Mrs Linton's washing in the servants' garden. As she closed her eyes to savour the moment, Edward strode into the garden, scaring her as he shouted "You! Get me some food!" Jane was unsure how to react because it was not her place to serve food to the master of the house and she feared she would be in dreadful bother if she did it, but in dreadful bother if she didn't.

A calm, soothing voice answered her prayers, "Edward, if you come in I'll have Elizabeth make us some lunch. Stop frightening little girls." Mrs Linton laughed as she re-traced her steps.

Edward stared at Jane. He knew he would have her before the night was out.

After everyone had gone to their beds, Edward spoke to Elizabeth, the Housekeeper, "There's a chill in the air and I feel I need the fire to be set away. Send up Jane, she's … efficient. I shall be in the oak bedroom."

Elizabeth nodded, understanding his request. She regretted sending such a sweet girl to be defiled by a morally corrupt man who would throw her aside once she was no longer chaste and innocent; but the sacrifice of one girl stood against the possible ruination of Elizabeth's entire family if she rebuffed his request.

Secure in the fact that his wife would not interrupt his lovemaking as he had told her he felt ill and needed the space of a room to himself to lay quietly and recover, Edward kissed her and said 'Goodnight' as he left and headed for the oak bedroom; she knew better than to argue.

Finding Jane, Elizabeth told her "Your presence is required in Mr Linton's room, the oak bedroom. He ... needs you to ... lay a fire."

Jane registered surprise at a fire after midnight, but set about gathering her bucket and tools to do just that. "Poor Mr Linton, he must be very cold. I should hurry."

"Yes, he is, he's a very cold person" said Elizabeth.

As Jane picked up her bucket, Elizabeth touched her shoulder. She looked drawn and sad as she reached to kiss Jane's forehead. A motherly urge to warn and maybe even protect Jane surged through Elizabeth, but self preservation won and she just smiled.

Edward, in his room, was becoming more excited by the minute. He wished the foolish, but beautiful and very pleasingly rounded girl, would hurry up. If she was worth his time he could have this little room as his guilty secret and Jane would be here whenever he wanted her attentions.

Jane knocked lightly on the door, the bucket was heavy with coal and sticks and fire tools and she was struggling to keep it upright. He told her to come in. She entered the room and made straight for the fireplace. As she bent to place the bucket on the hearth she felt his hands grope around her waist. She jumped up and turned to face him. Although Jane had never experienced any intimacy she knew intuitively what was about to happen. Her immediate response was to writhe out of his grasp but as his hands explored further and his breathing became deeper, she knew it was pointless to resist ... and, did she want to? In the seconds it took for Jane to decide to not only give in, but to respond, Edward was on his knees and grappling under her dress. Jane stepped backwards putting up one hand to slow him as she unbuttoned her bodice. Edward smiled and stepped back to watch. As the plainness of her maid's dress fell away to reveal the prize that Edward so desired, Jane prayed to God to forgive her and protect her.

It was a night of lust and passion. Jane was a willing partner to Edward's fervour. She had to admit that she had, for the most part, enjoyed her first foray into ... *love*.

As Edward indicated the end of the night by pushing Jane away and hissing "Get out!" she believed he was just over-tired and now needed to sleep. Indeed she was right, he was both of those things, but she also believed he would awaken and want her back by his side and he would be affectionate and gentle with her; but for now she should leave him. She tiptoed down stairs, passing through myriad corridors, to find Elizabeth.

"Oh Elizabeth, you'll never guess what happened!" Jane spoke as quietly as an excited young girl could.

"I think I can." said Elizabeth. "How are you feeling? You should lie down and let the pain drain away."

"What pain? I have no pain; well, it did hurt but not now. Elizabeth, Edward is such a wonderful man."

Elizabeth sighed; she'd seen it all before ... an innocent girl has her head turned by the lewd attentions of a powerful man. She offered what advice she could: 'don't tell anyone', 'just give in', 'don't be upset when he's tired of you'. Jane accepted the advice by nodding, but actually had not heard any of it; her thoughts were centred on this wonderful new sensation of 'love'. Elizabeth paused and peered at Jane. She realised that this time, this girl, was falling in love and hurtling towards disaster. She had to knock sense into this silly little girl before she got them all killed.

"Jane, it was one night! He just wanted you because you're innocent and because you're lovely but he does not love you. He never will. He has a wife! And he's a man of high standing; don't make him cross Jane, we could all suffer."

Jane was bemused by Elizabeth's reaction but she didn't have time to argue, it was one hour to getting up time and she now realised that she felt bone-weary, but yet quite excited, by the night's encounter.

THREE

Night after night Edward excused himself from the marital bed, after having satisfied his wife, to 'sleep alone'. It was so easy having Jane in the same house, it became a regular routine. Edward was having fun; Jane was open to suggestion when it came to discovering new ways to please him, and she was pretty, young and very biddable. But even these things become boring in the hands of the wrong person. Edward took Jane to unknown and frightening places where her body felt torn and her mind shut down. Because he loved her, as she thought, then she should be a willing partner but as the darkness of his nature came more to the fore, she retreated into her own shady place. In this place she could persuade herself that Edward only did these monstrous things because he loved her so much.

Edward was enjoying the delights of Betsy, a seasoned professional, whilst wallowing in the wonderful adoration of an unsuspecting, naive girl who was over-awed by his fame, his wealth, his power and his unrelenting carnal appetite.

Jane was unaware of just how powerful Edward was within the town. But she would learn.

The day arrived, of course, when Edward Linton did *not* call for Jane. She was distraught, "What's happened to him, Elizabeth?"

Elizabeth eyed her young friend and decided that letting her down gently was a waste of time. "He's bored now, Jane. He always gets bored. He must have bedded every girl in Darlington by now! He's a bastard and there's nowt you can do 'bout it. Get on with your jobs and forget him!"

"I'll go to his room and make sure he's not ill," said Jane, picking up her shawl as she made for the door.

"You will not! If *he* doesn't kill you, his wife *will*! Now stop this fuss and get to work!" Elizabeth did not look as though she could be argued with so Jane nodded and left the room.

Later, in the privacy of the servants' attic, Jane wrote a letter to Edward:

My Dear Edward,

You have not called for me in a while.

My body is yours, my heart is yours and my soul is yours. Will you call me to your room very soon?

Jane

She paid one of the young boys employed on the Bishop's estate to sneak her love letter to Edward whilst he was out walking. However, in her eagerness to have the note delivered she had forgotten to insist that it should only be handed to Edward and no one else. The messenger, in his youth and ignorance, handed the wretched letter to Edward's wife! She showed her rage that night in bed. *This Jane was the latest in a very long and embarrassingly hurtful line of young girls who had shared her husband's body. This Jane would be the last!*

When Edward arrived home his wife behaved as lovingly as she could and, with hardly any effort, she lured him to their bedroom. As the night took its usual turn towards consensual depravity, she paused him, saying that she was feeling rather dizzy from the pure enjoyment of what was to come and would he mind getting her some water, all the while suggesting that tonight she intended to match his desire for perversion.

He grudgingly rolled out of bed and walked, naked, to the adjoining room to find the water jug. His wife jumped up and ran to the windowsill where she had hidden a surprise for Edward, something that should appeal to his sense of torturous decadence. She hid it just beneath the edge of the bed. When he returned she smiled wantonly, saying, "I feel better. You lie down now and close your eyes and I'll make you scream with delight." Edward lay down, smiling, and closed his eyes. He didn't have long to wait. As his wife stood over him, she whispered "This came from Jane." Edward screamed then passed out as a hot iron was pressed onto his groin and left there to sear its message onto his brain.

FOUR

The town gossip was that Edward Linton, Darlington's Major General, had had an accident and was now confined to his bed. Apparently he'd tripped and fallen, in his home, and had the misfortune to land on a smoothing iron! Some nasty burns had resulted and it would be a while before he could walk again; there were some things he would *never* do again.

Edward's wife had not yet finished her work; she also had a surprise for his mistress. She spoke to the Bishop about Jane and confessed to him that when her husband 'fell' onto the iron, the spirit of Jane had appeared in the room and pushed him directly onto it. She said Edward had identified the witch-like spirit to be Jane and he was now afraid of the spirit returning to kill him; for good measure, she pointed out that Jane was Catholic.

The Bishop visited Edward, to bless him, and during that meeting he asked "Edward, I have to ask you about that night. Think carefully before you answer. Did the spirit of Jane Atkinson appear in your house and cause this awful accident?" Under threat of further public humiliation by his wife, Edward nodded "Yes, it was Jane. She will come back and kill me! She's a witch!" Having agreed that the spirit of Jane had been the cause of his downfall he thought it wise to also confess to having had countless debauched encounters with Jane, but only because she had beguiled him.

"Please Bishop, ask God's forgiveness for my transgressions and help to save my soul from this witch's claws!"

Bishop Grace was shocked, but secretly delighted, to have a witch within his own household. He blessed Edward and assured him that God had forgiven him and punished him and it would now be his own pleasure to do God's bidding in trying Jane as a witch.

Bishop Grace had never actually conducted a witch trial, although he knew of them. He had been told of a very efficient and holy man living in Scotland, called Cuthbert Nicholson, who was a Witch-Finder. It was his job, his duty, his pleasure, to find witches and dispose of them. It was God's will. It's very difficult to argue against God's will. So, no one did.

The Witch-Finder was delighted to be invited to serve God in Darlington; finding witches had proven to be very lucrative, a high price being paid for each witch who was subsequently put to death. Cuthbert Nicholson, on God's behalf, ordered Jane to be arrested and secured to a tabletop. Her bodice was required to be removed, though no one was quite sure why, and her face covered. The Witch-Finder took his time examining Jane's upper body. He then pulled up her skirt and pressed a large needle into her thigh; she didn't react to the needle no matter how deeply it was plunged into her skin – this was a sure sign of a witch, they feel no pain and they do not bleed. Unsuspecting eyewitnesses had failed to spot the needlepoint as it drew back into the handle, thereby never touching Jane's flesh. Having finished his trickery the Witch-Finder called his henchmen to take Jane away. He returned his retractable witch-finding needle to its case and went back to the Bishop's Palace for a banquet in his honour.

FIVE

Jane languished in a filthy squalid cell in Bridewell Gaol in Durham. The walls ran with slime; slime that had a smell of its own, a disgusting, stomach-wrenching smell that made you feel as though you had actually licked the wall and swallowed the glutinous mass that fell onto your tongue. It was not unknown for prisoners to do just that because after days of starvation and dehydration, most people would do anything. Leg irons were clamped around Jane's thin ankles ... but not before the gaolers had made sure she enjoyed her stay, such a pretty young thing deserved to have *that* pleasure. Straw was thrown onto the floor to suffice as a bed, a little luxury that did not make up for the stench that came from the fact that there was no sewer and waste was only removed fortnightly. During her stay at Durham Jane ate only 'water soup', a dish served up by her gaolers because bread boiled in water was the tastiest, and cheapest, meal they could make. It wasn't nourishing but, unfortunately, it kept her alive.

Not only was Jane being accused of witchcraft, but she was now also known to be Catholic. Times had changed since Jane was a child; it was now forbidden to pray and go to Church, under threat of death. Her fate was sealed and she could do nothing to save herself. Her family, including her beloved mother, disowned her for fear of bringing retribution onto themselves.

So, alone she sat, alone she cried, alone she prayed.

Day after day went by, leaving Jane time to ponder not only how she had come to this but how she might cope with the coming terror. From tales her mother had told her, it would not end well. She knew about people who had been accused of heresy or witchcraft and she comforted herself with the thought that none of them had been in Darlington, and it was all so long ago, surely things had changed since the 1590s.

Her mother's voice rang in her ears "We always need t'be careful, Jane, don't upset any one and don't let on 'bout being Catholic, you can get killed for it. Say your prayers in your head. Some Priests were killed round here you know. Long time ago, like, but you never know. That Cromwell, he doesn't like us."

She heard her own voice, in reply "How d'they kill Priests?"

"It's horrible, Jane, the poor Priest is hung, but before he dies they cut him down." This didn't seem too bad to the young Jane, more a punishment than a death. "Then while he's still alive they cut him up *and* they pull bits out! Sometimes they boil the bits! Then ... they stick his head on a pole!"

Jane's face began to crumple as she imagined the scene. Just as her stomach was threatening to empty itself, her mother noticed the pallor on her daughter's face and quickly spoke of things less threatening, "... but we don't need to worry about that! Come on, we *do* need to tidy this house though! Then, you can help me with the baking."

Jane knew all about John Boste and John Ingram, who had died for their faith, in Durham; however, she had overheard the gaolers talking and they had said the Bishop was having her taken back to Darlington. A sense of relief flooded through her mangled mind and eased her broken body because in Darlington people were not put to death.

She had forgotten about George Swallowell; executed in Darlington town centre and whose remains were buried under the Market Square!

SIX

Having lost count of how many days she had spent in Bridewell Gaol, how many times she had been raped and beaten, how many times she had felt starvation grab at her stomach, Jane realised that her only relief lay in God. She prayed and she prayed but no Divine Body came to take her hand and lead her away to everlasting peace. But ... someone else was offering her a better path; someone else was planting an idea into her broken-hearted, melancholy brain. And Jane was listening.

One morning Jane was awakened by the sound of her cell door being opened. Edward's men had come to take her back to Darlington. She was a very sorry sight, having lain for weeks in faeces-covered straw and bearing the telltale signs of utter neglect and abuse; unwashed, unwanted, unloved. She was leashed to the back of a cart, around which had gathered a crowd of merciless onlookers who hit her at every opportunity, they spat at her and called for her death. The cart moved very slowly along the pitted track and Jane followed, the rope tied tightly at the wrist, almost forcing her hands into the prayer-form. After two miles the soldiers stopped to throw a very tired, despairing Jane onto the cart.

The cart came to a halt in Darlington market place, next to the stocks. To ensure that Jane-the-witch did not fly off she was secured into the stocks while charges against her were read aloud to a jeering audience. After the charges of 'witchcraft and trickery' and 'causing much harm to the esteemed Edward Linton' were declared, the mob was invited to throw stones, food, gravel, anything at all, at Jane. She closed her eyes but would not dip down her head in shame or fear. A new strength was coursing through her and she knew she could resist all attempts to quell her spirit. A soft voice very close to her ear brought her back to consciousness. "Jane, my name is Betsy. I ... I know Edward. And I know you didn't do anything. I know what he's like, he's a wicked man."

Jane wanted to see Betsy. With half-opened eyes she strained to take in the lovely face before her. "Jane, I'll stay with you. We're the same, me and you ... I know it could be me in these stocks" and Betsy reached to clasp one of Jane's filthy and bloody hands. Betsy's brave gesture of friendship and understanding filled Jane's heart with happiness and she smiled weakly as her fingers tried to squeeze Betsy's hand. "God will look after you, Jane." Jane really had to smile at that.

An hour passed before Jane was dragged around the market place, down to Prebends Row then onto Northgate to the pond that served that part of town. There she was secured into the ducking stool, which had only ever been used as punishment for minor crimes, so today was a big day.

As the stool swung over the water the crowd hushed; Jane moaned, even half conscious she knew what was coming. The first ducking was enough to leave her gasping for air. Standing on the pond-side, Betsy was distraught. She knew Jane was innocent but she was too terrified to speak out, to describe the many injuries she had received at the hands of Edward Linton. Betsy shuddered as she spied Edward coming through the crowd; he limped, being now permanently disabled and disfigured.

SEVEN

The ducking stool went under for the second time. This time it stayed down a little longer – just to give Jane a fair chance to prove that she really was not a witch.

"Bring it up slowly, lads!" shouted Edward. Up came a limp, lifeless Jane. The mindless mob found it's conscience for a moment and felt a twinge of guilt as one of them observed "My God! She was innocent!"

As the mob turned away in silence, shamed but yet a little disappointed, Jane made the second biggest mistake of her life.

She moved.

Edward had noticed the movement and was swift to react: "Ahhh! She's alive! She **IS** a witch! I heard her uttering satanic curses!" he squealed delightedly. The mob stopped and turned as one. Each heartbeat quickening, all trace of guilt evaporating.

"Down! Down! Down!" they screamed in crescendo as Jane started to regain consciousness. Poor Jane, They waited for her to become fully aware before they proceeded with their awful deed.

But by the third ducking Jane wanted to die. She knew that if she lived a worse fate awaited her. Burning at the stake was infinitely more horrible than drowning. Her eyes had now lost that desperate look and she had long since ceased to declare her innocence.

As the ducking stool hit the water for its third and final journey, Jane gazed sadly across the pond into the eyes of the accursed Edward. She would take his gaze with her to her grave. He too would remember that gaze...

Edward wanted no more of Jane Atkinson. She must die. He motioned for the stool to be held down; long enough so that no one could survive.

When they finally raised the stool, Jane was dead.

Betsy, unable to control her rising emotions, ran off in the direction of home, to release the tears and the anguish.

The mob felt a little cheated; they had prepared the market place for a burning. Jane's body was loosened from its bondage as the mob drifted away. Morbid curiosity beckoned a small crowd to watch as she was taken from the stool and tossed carelessly onto a waiting cart. The observers huddled around, some even dared to prod the lifeless body, hoping that she would spring up and take flight.

"Take her to the market place! Burn her body anyway!" said Edward, pleased with his day's work.

He stopped. Did he see Jane's eyes flicker open for a second?

No, impossible.

"Go on then! Do it! Now!" he shouted, trying to hide the rising panic.

"Well, Mr Linton, are you going back home now?" enquired the Bishop, who had come along to ensure that fair play was adhered to. As they talked, clouds of smoke arose from the market place followed by a ringing cheer. Edward felt only relief.

"Erm, no. I think I'll take a walk out. You know, blow away the cobwebs". With that he walked away, abruptly ending the conversation and headed towards the open land between the market place and the Bishop's Palace. He needed to get home and lie down.

The Bishop shouted after him "We have a lot to thank you for today, Mr Linton! Hadn't been for you we wouldn't have known *anything* about Jane Atkinson! God Bless you!"

EIGHT

The daytime sun was receding as Edward walked; a feeling of dread wormed its uneasy path around his body until it felt as though every nerve was tingling with horrible anticipation. Secluded, but beautiful, the land stretched before him. Now he would walk and breathe in the view of the lingering River Skerne gently meandering around the town. He would cleanse his soul.

Deeply hurt by his betrayal, Jane would exact her own revenge upon the man who had torn out her heart.

Edward Linton had entered her life and turned it upside down. Foolishly she had offered herself to him body and soul. He took what he wanted and then discarded her. To Jane the affair was total and all-absorbing. Brutal hands taught her about the raging, perverse nature of love.

Edward looked around; the air was alive with memories.

His memories.

Jane's memories.

Deep feelings had stirred within Jane when she surveyed the hauntingly desolate surroundings of her birth; the place she loved. Edward was no romantic though; he scrutinised the land and anticipated the wealth to be had from selling off vast swathes to be urbanised. He was, of course, assuming that Cromwell would reward him with local land, having proved himself to be a model Major General. Smiling as he considered his own good fortune, not counting the iron, Edward felt invigorated and set off. Contentment flowed through his veins.

A faint moan disturbed his reverie.

Must be the wind.

A strange stillness surrounded Edward. He was finding it increasingly difficult to walk. A great force was barring his way, impeding his progress. Mist emerging from the earth, gave rise to undefined shapes swirling about in its murky midst. Walking towards him, a shadow at first, was Jane, speaking in her low timorous voice.

"You killed me, Edward. All I ever did was love you ... and you killed me."

Weeping as she spoke, tears swept down her face, burning holes in her dress as they fell.

"Now Edward, you owe me your life. Come to me Edward."

"No! No! God help me! I ... I ... I saw you drown! They burned you! How did you get here?" Choking on his words, Edward stumbled backwards, trying desperately to escape.

"Edward, surely you didn't really think you could kill me. You can take away the mortal frame, Edward, but the spirit lives!"

With these words, she laughed. The dark hair, once so captivating, transformed into slimy, sticky pondweed. Her beautiful face distorted – the eyes bulging from their sockets, straining to be released; the finely carved cheekbones swelled and cracked; the pouting lips turned blue and shrivelled whilst the smooth creamy skin discoloured to almost black.

Incredulous, Edward breathed his final words.

"You *are* a witch!"

Jane fixed him with her sad gaze.

"No, Edward, I'm no witch. But when you sent me under water for the last time I made a pact with the Devil.

"He could have *my* soul as long as I could have *yours*!"

Feeling his body being torn apart, Edward screamed.

A scream that would echo through eternity.

END

The Secrets of 24 Blackwellgate - Book One

"These two linked stories touch on the
social mores of the 19th. Century, with
some time travelling thrown in
for good measure.
They are dedicated to special people and places,
gone too soon."
~Beryl

A GHOST AT THE DOOR:
(Sarah's Story)

'we met across time'

THE HOMECOMING:
(Simon's Story)

'love exists in many guises.
Remember that all that really matters is love itself'

The Secrets of 24 Blackwellgate - Book One

"She looked about twenty years of age, had dishevelled light brown hair, was slim and extremely pretty. Apart from the slightly awry old fashioned maid's cap and thin unbuttoned cotton top she was wearing, which were totally unsuitable for the weather outside, the most striking thing about her was the sheer panic in her wide expressive hazel eyes."

A GHOST AT THE DOOR

Part 1:

It was just before Christmas 2014.
We were very busy in our shop, which was why it was a few moments before I noticed her standing in front of me.
When I did, the sight of the girl sent a tingle up my spine.
She looked about twenty years of age, had dishevelled light brown hair, was slim and extremely pretty.
Apart from the slightly awry old-fashioned maid's cap and thin unbuttoned cotton top she was wearing, which were totally unsuitable for the weather outside, the most striking thing about her was the sheer panic in her wide expressive hazel eyes.
"Let me go downstairs," she pleaded. "That monster must not find me."
There was something about the urgency of her request that made me do as she wished.
I had just shut the basement door behind her, and through the glass panel in it seen her scurrying down the steep steps when quite violently the front door blew open, and the whole place went icy cold.
A dark shadow was cast on the floor, which then receded as suddenly as it had appeared, but no one came inside.
Shoppers were looking towards the entrance to see what had happened.
I walked over and closed the door.
A man browsing greetings cards nearby said, "What on earth was that?"
"Just a freak gust of wind I expect," said I, although I wasn't convinced.
As soon as I could I went downstairs, eager to see what our unexpected guest was all about.

There was no one there, so I assumed the girl had opened the safety doors and made her escape out of the back exit.
Except that when I checked the bolts they were all still in place.
The only other explanation was that whilst I was closing the front door, she had come back upstairs and mingled with the other people and eventually left without me noticing her.
I contented myself with that.
A short time later that same day, I took a customer into the basement, which is stuffed with retro bits and bobs.
Suddenly she said, "I hope you don't mind me saying this, but I have a gift which sometimes puts me in touch with the spirit world and I sense at least one presence down here."
Feeling that same tingle in my spine, which I had experienced when I saw the girl who had asked to go into our basement, I timidly asked, "Is it a young woman?"
The lady replied, "It is indeed, but she's not alone. I can see a girl kneeling in front of a middle-aged female, who's seated on a carved wooden chair. They're near the old range over there. Their clothing looks to be Victorian. They're holding onto each other and they seem to be very afraid."
I shivered as I took in her words, and felt a little dizzy.
For a moment, I actually thought I saw those figures too, and blinked in disbelief.
It must have been my imagination playing tricks, as when I opened my eyes again the fleeting vision was gone.
I felt very strange and unreal.
The customer's hand on my arm steadying me, and her voice saying, "I hope I haven't frightened you, but the spirits won't harm you, you know," jolted me back to reality.
She continued, "having said that, I sense we are not welcome just now, so perhaps we should leave."
I obliged with alacrity and was back up those stairs in what seemed like a flash.

The woman followed me carrying the armful of items she had chosen and said, "If you want me to come back and do a proper investigation, I will."
She put her contact details on a scrap of paper, and thrust it into my shaking hand, then paid for her purchases and left.

Part 2:

Several weeks had passed since that day, which annoyingly enough had also been the anniversary of the day I was born, the twenty-third of December.
I'd tried not to let what had happened spoil my birthday or the Christmas celebrations, by telling myself that the 'sighting' or whatever it was, had been nothing but a load of old bunkum made up by a crank.
The only trouble was that for a crank the lady in question had seemed remarkably sane at the time.
Due to having to concentrate on the day to day running of the business, after a while I almost completely got over her claim that there were Victorian apparitions inhabiting our basement, and just got on with life.
It was March and that meant it was stocktaking time.
As nothing further had happened to spook me, I'd started to be able to go downstairs on my own again without having a panic attack, so that was good.
I really liked it down there. It was quaint and interesting and seemed to have regained its nice atmosphere.
I volunteered for the job of counting the stock below stairs, as it was deemed to be my special interest part of the shop.
After all, it was me who had suggested calling that particular department, 'The Fabulous Flea Pit'.
The stocktaking was progressing well. I had the radio tuned to Steve Wright's show, and was smiling at the banter and singing along happily to his playlist as I carefully counted everything,

and then I saw it. It was a faded pencil drawing on thick card, of a female face.

On closer inspection I saw that the face strongly resembled that of the girl I had seen three months earlier, and whom I had allowed down here into the deepest part of the building. I was stunned.

It was propped up on the mantelshelf above the old range, as though someone had deliberately set it there to make sure I didn't miss it.

My heart skipped a beat, and I thought, 'Oh my God, just what is happening here, am I going crazy?'

I instinctively glanced sideways in the direction of the spot where the customer who professed to be psychic had claimed to have seen the two figures, and thankfully there was nothing there.

'This must be some kind of joke,' I thought.

I work with three other people and when I told them about my find they said it was nothing to do with them, and suggested that maybe the mysterious girl I'd told them about had left it there herself, and we just hadn't noticed it until now.

I accepted that theory but made sure I had a few glasses of rum after work, so that I could blot the whole thing out. The next day I went back downstairs to finish the counting, and my eyes immediately went to that likeness of the girl which was still in the place I had left it, but now placed neatly by the hearth as if someone had put them there to warm, I saw a pair of old-fashioned shoes, made from ivory kid leather. We source quite a few examples of antique accessories and clothing for the shop, but I couldn't recall acquiring these. They did look familiar however, and I felt physically sick when I realised I had glimpsed some very similar shoes, if not the same ones, on the feet of the scared girl as she scooped up her long skirts and scampered down our stairs.

That was it. I called the lady who had told me she was a medium.

Part 3:

Irene Sangster said she would come to see me that very day. She had been very nice when I rang her.
I think she sensed the trepidation in my voice as I reminded her of her visit to our shop and of what she had told me she had seen, and how it had affected me.
I told her about the girl, about the shadow on the threshold and about the further developments.
I also confessed that the whole thing was freaking me out, which was why I was taking her up on the offer she had made to investigate further.
True to her word she arrived bang on two o'clock, as promised.
The friends who I work with were sceptical, but recognising that I was troubled by something they couldn't explain away they reluctantly went along with it all.
My colleague Colin made everyone hot drinks, and the medium and I took ours downstairs.
Mrs. Sangster, on reaching the bottom of the stairs looked into the room containing the old fire range and nodded acknowledgment to someone or something I couldn't see.
I started to have misgivings.
'The woman obviously is mad after all,' I thought.
Unperturbed and looking satisfied she remarked, "that's good, we are welcome today."
She then asked to see the portrait. She looked closely at it and said, "A very pretty face," then turned it over to see if there was anything written on the back which would give us any clues, but finding nothing remarked, "now, what about these

shoes?"

She examined the footwear carefully.

The shoes were beautifully hand made in once pristine ivory kid, but the pale soft leather was stained and ragged now. They were small in size, very narrow with lowish heels and each shoe had a cheeky little bow trim on the front of it.

"A young girl's shoes," she said "perhaps even wedding shoes, and just look at the makers name and address inside them, they were made by someone called A Wheeler in this very building, number 24, Blackwellgate."

Part 4:

After leaving The Friends Meeting House, a Quaker establishment where she liked to go to help out, Sarah Susannah Wheeler headed for home.

She didn't have far to go, as her home was just around the corner.

Her family, in spite of being good industrious people, had fallen on hard times since her father Arthur had taken ill and could no longer make the shoes, which had always kept them in modest comfort.

He was a good shoemaker, and his work had been much acclaimed by the more discerning amongst the population of Darlington.

His last real job had been to make Sarah a pretty pair of ivory kid court shoes for her eighteenth birthday, but after that he struggled as cancer took its course.

With Arthur Wheeler now unable to work, any money the family had put by was gradually dwindling away.

Sarah had a brother, and if he had only done what most sons might have done and followed his father's trade, then things would have been easier for the family.

As it was Simon Wheeler was restless and adventurous and had left the family home saying he was going to sea

He had returned only once since then, to let his family know that he was now living and working in Whitby, which was the hometown of his pregnant lass.

That news had caused a terrible row, during which his father had accused Simon of deserting the family trade, fathering a baby out of wedlock and bringing them into disrepute.

Arthur himself had been relatively mature when he had married the much younger Barbara, and became a father late in life.

This was partly why conflict between father and son had arisen in the first place, as the older man being set in his ways could not quite cope with his son's desire to break with tradition.

On top of that Arthur's illness was progressing rapidly.

Pain and fear added to his anger, but he was too proud to tell his son this, so harsh things were said on both sides that day.

The result was that Simon left again, in total ignorance of the true state of affairs, vowing never to return.

That made Sarah very sad as she loved her big brother very much, and she knew he loved her too.

She remembered what a keen artist he was and how he used to try to make her sit still so that he could draw her, and how much she used to fidget and protest.

If only he was here now she would be happy to sit as still as a mouse for him.

As she walked home she reflected on all of this, and on the financial difficulties her family were struggling with since her father had been forced to give in to his illness.

She had thought of trying to get to Whitby to let her brother know of their plight, as surely he would help.

Whitby however, was a long way away, and it would be folly for a young girl to try the trip on her own.

In any case, she didn't even have an address for him and for all she knew he and his Grace could have moved on.
A tear ran down her cheek, as she feared for what would become of them all.

Part 5:

On a dull autumn day in 1873 Arthur Wheeler passed away. He was buried a week later in the Quaker cemetery which was tucked away behind Skinnergate.
The group of mourners who stood around the grave were truly sorry to bid this good man a final farewell.
Sarah looked down at her feet on which she wore the shoes her father had made especially for her. In her mind, she could hear the words he had used when he proudly presented them to her the day she turned eighteen, "Here my sweet Sarah, I made these for thee to wear on thy wedding day, but I want to give them to thee now. I hope they will serve thee well."
Privately she'd hoped her wedding day would not come for some time, as she didn't want to marry simply for reasons of material security. She didn't let her parents know that of course, and graciously accepted the shoes, which were then stored away safely in a special box.
She had worn them today in honour of the man who made them and would wear them frequently from now on, as keeping footwear in storage was a luxury that could no longer be afforded.
With her father gone, Sarah knew that so much would now be changed. At that moment, it would have been a great comfort to have her brother by her side.
The previous month, when Arthur's illness had taken a turn for the worse a message had been dispatched to the only address in Whitby they knew, that of an acquaintance who had moved there years back. The message asked the friend to look for

Simon Wheeler to let him know that Arthur was dying, but there had been no word back.

They prayed Simon might have received the bad news and been moved to return in time for this ceremony, but he never appeared.

So, Barbara and Sarah sadly went back home alone.

Being the good folk that they were their own relations and the other Quaker families now gathered round to help as much as they could. One of Arthur Wheeler's best customers for shoes had been a shopkeeper called Mrs Thorpe. After a decent time had elapsed she and her husband called on Barbara and Sarah, who were now in greatly reduced circumstances and in imminent danger of losing their home.

Partly to help the bereaved mother and daughter, and partly because it was a lovely place to live and do business, they offered to take over the rent of Number 24.

This would be done on the understanding that the Thorpe's, who were childless, would live above the shop and Barbara and Sarah would move below stairs, and be expected to do the domestic chores such as cooking and sewing. Sarah was expected to help in the shop at busy times too.

The retail area of course would continue to be sited on the ground floor, but now would sell Mrs Thorpe's drapery items instead of being the place where Mr Wheeler made and sold his shoes.

In return for their work Barbara and Sarah would get a small wage, a roof over their heads, and their keep.

It was a drastic upheaval for them, but they had no option but to accept.

Once rent arrears, business debtors, medical and funeral costs and so on had been paid, there was hardly anything left.

Barbara Wheeler who was now in her late forties missed her gentle husband very much and wore mainly black from the day

of his death onwards, which made her look much older than her years.
She also missed her son, but she did have Sarah so she accepted her lot, and was thankful for having such a supportive daughter close at hand.
That was to change very soon.
Once the days' work was done, the widow Wheeler's favourite place to rest was on a high backed chair near the fire, which crackled in the grate of the big black-leaded range. This room containing the range, doubled as Barbara's and Sarah's living room and the kitchen for the whole household. They both slept in a second smaller room, which was just across a little stairwell.
Access to these rooms, was made by descending a flight of stone steps which led to that stairwell, from the shop.
The front room of their quarters was a proper underground cellar but as the land in that area fell away sharply, the back room where they slept was not underground at all.
In fact there was a back door in the stairwell, and behind that door was a short passageway, leading out onto Houndgate.
The floor of this basement accommodation was flagged throughout and even in the summer if the fire was not lit it could get a little damp and chilly down there, but as the fire almost always was on for hot water and cooking, it wasn't really a problem.

Part 6:

The real problem arose when Mr Thorpe left home.
One night after they had finished most of their work and were settling down by the fire together, not for the first time Sarah and her mother heard raised voices coming from upstairs.
This time, it seemed different.
There was a floor between them, but the argument was so

fierce that although they couldn't quite make out the words, it was obvious that something very serious was going on.

Sarah had known that the master of the house was out a great deal, and it was rumoured that he was enamoured by a pretty young barmaid at the tavern a couple of doors down from where they lived.

This was scandalous behaviour for a gentleman, especially in a largely Quaker town. Nevertheless, it seemed the man was smitten.

The commotion moved down to the ground floor, and now the
Inhabitants of the basement could hear what was being said.

"Leave go of me you miserable woman," boomed Mr Thorpe's gruff voice.

His wife was sobbing, "please don't leave me. Think of the shame your desertion will bring on us."

He resisted her pleas saying, "It is too late madam. The fault lies in you. If you had lavished as much attention on me, as you have on business then this would never have happened."

Then the front door slammed and the gentleman had gone.

Once the dust had settled the Thorpe's didn't go as far as divorce, but referred to their new relationship amongst their acquaintances as, "A necessary separation."

Lizzie Thorpe clung to the hope that this arrangement meant there was still a chance that her husband might come back.

It was agreed between them that she would be allocated an allowance from her husband, and be able to carry on her business alone.

This meant that she was reasonably well provided for, due to the income from her drapers shop, but it did mean that that she would have to make some cutbacks, and one of those turned out to be Sarah's keep.

"Sarah my dear," said the lady of the house, "I can't afford to feed and lodge you any longer, but you are a good girl, and I

have found you a wonderful position as a lady's maid. I am so sorry, but you are to start with your new family tomorrow."
Barbara and Sarah were horrified, but had no choice other than to accept the situation.
Mother and daughter spent a tearful, sleepless night, after being given this news.
The first thing the next day they packed a trunk in readiness for Sarah to move out.
"Have courage," Barbara told her beloved child.
Sarah mustered a brave smile, and answered, "I will miss you so much but I'm not going far, and hope I will be able to return as often as possible."
Then this thoughtful girl placed the treasured drawing of herself which her brother had done just before he left, on the mantelshelf saying, "see mother, I will still be here with you in spirit."
Sad as this new development made them feel, they had no idea what further trials lay ahead.

Part 7:

A servant had been sent with a barrow to transport Sarah's belongings to their new home. He was a sullen looking young man and didn't speak unless spoken to on the short journey to a rather grand house known as Chorley Hall. The hall stood alone at the town end of the tree-lined road leading to the villages of High and Low Coniscliffe.
Joseph, which Sarah had managed to discover was the fellow's name, took Sarah's luggage to the back door of the house.
He heaved her trunk from the barrow and dumped it on the ground, then rapped on the knocker.
The heavy tongue and grooved wooden door opened to reveal a sturdy, red-cheeked servant girl.
"Ah, you must be Sarah, we were expecting you," the girl said

with a grin.

Sarah felt relieved to be greeted by a friendly face and smiled back.

"I'm Polly," she continued, "you and me will be sharing a bed."

Polly then took hold of one of the handles of Sarah's trunk and said, "come on Joe, let's get this upstairs, and then I'll show Sarah around."

The three of them went up the narrow creaky back staircase, which was the route the servants used to access the upper floors.

Sarah followed behind with her hand luggage whilst the other two, who led the way, struggled with their heavy load up the three floors to the attic rooms, where the servants slept.

Once the trunk was safely deposited up there Joe left them to it. After helping her unpack a few things, Polly took Sarah downstairs again to meet the housekeeper, as instructed.

"That will be all Polly," said Mrs Jones.

She then beckoned to Sarah to come through into the main part of the house.

They entered a large panelled room with a high and beautifully plastered ceiling, many fine paintings on the walls and sumptuous velvet drapes.

The occupant of this fine space was seated on a window seat seemingly oblivious of her opulent surroundings, her head bowed over the book she was reading.

Sarah felt very nervous as she approached, but as she drew near the lady looked up, and the girl saw that this woman who was now her mistress had kind eyes and a sorrowful but sweet expression on her face, and her fear evaporated.

Mrs Jones announced, "the new girl Sarah, Mrs Nicholson."

Sarah dipped a little curtsy, as her mother had advised her to do.

Mrs Jones had left the room, and the two of them were now

alone."
Eleanor Nicholson put down her book with an approving look. In a soft melodic voice the lady explained, "I have been quite ill for some while and my weakened state has caused me to become rather morose, so I felt I might benefit from engaging a companion from outside this house, to distract me."
"My draper Mrs Thorpe told me that you would be well suited to the post and I feel she was right. I am sure that you and I will get along very well indeed."
Then she became very serious and leaned forward to say something which Sarah found strange, "This may prove to be a temporary position, and the one thing you have to remember is that should anything happen to me you must immediately return to your own home."

Part 8:

The days and weeks went on pleasantly enough, with Sarah helping her employer to wash and dress, bringing her meals, accompanying her on shopping trips to town, walking with her in the garden on the warmer days, conversing with her, reading to her in the evenings and helping her to bed at night.
The two of them, in spite of their different ages and stations in life were starting to become what can only be described as, friends.
Summer arrived and the house and grounds seemed to come alive.
When she was not tending to her lady, Sarah used to like to be outside, exploring the gardens, picking flowers for the house, playing on the lawn with the housekeepers cat, searching in the barn for stray hens eggs and just enjoying the warmth of the sun on her back.
It felt good to be alive. She smiled a lot because things had not worked out so badly after all.

The Secrets of 24 Blackwellgate - Book One

Mrs Nicholson, although not a Quaker herself, had no objection to Sarah walking the quarter mile to The Friends Meeting House every Sunday to worship in her own way, and was happy for her to spend time with her mother on that day too.
After the main quiet and reflective part of the meeting was over, Sarah and Barbara would break the silence to talk and drink tea with their fellow worshippers for a while, before going back to the basement rooms in Blackwellgate to share a precious hour or so alone together.
Sarah loved these Sundays and was very grateful for the time off to enjoy them, but she always made sure she set off back to the hall when the town clock struck five, in order to attend to her evening duties.
She would never have forgiven herself if she thought she had let her mistress down.
Attached to the Nicholson household were nine souls.
Mrs Eleanor Nicholson the lady of the house, Meg Jones the housekeeper and her son Joseph the odd job lad, Polly the parlour maid, Ada the scullery maid, Martha the cook, Sarah herself and the absent Mr James Nicholson and his son James junior, who everyone referred to as Jimmy.
There was little frivolity or unnecessary conversation between the staff, as everyone seemed intent on getting on with their own work.
In spite of this, Sarah got on well with them all, even Joe, who was hard working, and who on further acquaintance had proved to be shy and withdrawn rather than sullen as she had first thought.
The rumour was that for some reason Joe did not care for Mr Nicholson, due to something that had happened years back.
Sarah was too polite to enquire what that something was.
Sarah had been living amongst them for months now, and often wondered why the others hardly ever spoke of their master,

although she had heard many affectionate mentions of his son, but again she didn't like to pry.

Then one cold November night as she and Polly were snuggled up in the big double bed they shared Sarah plucked up the courage to ask, "Is the master a good man?"

Polly's normally rosy cheeks paled, as she answered, "you can soon judge for yourself, I heard mistress telling Mrs Jones that Mr Nicholson and master Jimmy are returning to spend Christmas here. They arrive at the end of this month."

This made Sarah feel uneasy, as it would inevitably mean change.

The month rolled on and with each day the atmosphere in the house seemed to darken as if something unsettling was imminent.

A day prior to the expected return of the master and his son, she discovered an answer to the question she had put to Polly. Her last job of the day, as usual, was to assist Mrs Nicholson into bed, and on this particular night she couldn't help but notice that her employer was distracted.

The lady seemed to be trying to make a decision about some troubling matter, which was on her mind.

Suddenly the she grasped both of Sarah's hands tightly in hers, saying, "Sarah, you must leave as soon as you can, it was selfish of me to bring you here at all," and then some upsetting truths began to pour out.

By the time Eleanor Nicholson had finished speaking, Sarah was in possession of, if not quite the whole story, some outrageous facts causing her to feel both fearful and protective at the same time.

Even though she knew as an employee she should not be so familiar, she threw her arms around Mrs Nicholson and held her tight as the poor lady sobbed uncontrollably. Eventually, exhausted by her emotions, Eleanor lay back on her pillows and fell asleep to dream disturbing dreams of things she had kept to herself for decades, but had just now related out loud to her trusted companion.

Part 9:

Eleanor was back in Chichester where she had been born. The year was 1851.
She was hardly more than a child again, reliving that horrible time after her mother had passed away from tuberculosis and then only months later being told that her father had been killed in a riding accident.
The solicitor's voice droned on in her head informing her that on her father's death as his only child she had inherited a large fortune, which would remain in trust until she came of age.
She didn't want that money she just wanted her parents back. Overcome with grief she let others decide what would happen next as she herself didn't really care much.
"This house needs to be sold and you must move to London to become the ward of your father's sister Lillian," the attorney continued.
Then her mind drifted out of the dream, only to return to it moments later.
A year had passed since the tragedies and she was now seventeen.
Sitting quietly reading in a favourite place of hers, the window seat in the drawing room hidden away behind the heavy red curtains was one of her only pleasures. She felt safe there.
People had entered the room, and she heard her aunt say, "I want my brother's child off my hands as quickly as possible. She's no fun, and makes the house gloomy with her stricken face and constant tears. I will happily marry her off to the next acceptable suitor who comes calling."
The family solicitor replied, "I think I know just the man."
As if through a mist she saw herself in a beautiful gown taking

part in a wedding ceremony, and then leaving as Mrs James Nicholson, on the arm of an older man whom she hardly knew.
She was in Darlington now living in her husband's family home. James, a wealthy banker, was about to take a trip back to London to keep control of where his money, and now also some of hers, was being invested.
He pulled her close to him saying, "be sure that I will hurry back."
She felt the seeds of hope rekindling in her.
Time passed, and Eleanor allowed herself to believe that happiness might be possible.
She was pregnant and James was leaving again.
"Business trip," he had told her, then added, "but I will be back here in time for the birth."
The birth was difficult and she was writhing in pain.
Soon the pain was a memory and was replaced by a feeling of contentment as she cradled a strong newborn boy to her breast.
She could see and hear her beaming husband saying, "Our first son shall be called James, but we will know him as Jimmy."
She now recalled happy times when they both focussed their attention on their child and spent a lot of time together as a family.
James put Jimmy's name down to go to the same private boarding school that he had attended, so Eleanor was making the most of these early years.
She found James very attentive. A little too attentive she began to think, as he became physically more and more demanding, asking her to do things she wasn't totally happy with.
Eleanor was with child again.
She relived the anguish she had felt when this baby, a girl, didn't survive more than a few days, falling prey to a fever.
Another pregnancy soon followed but Eleanor miscarried at

three months.

During her fourth pregnancy she was constantly feeling ill, so enquired of Doctor Bell if all the nocturnal attention from her husband might jeopardise their chance of a successful birth this time.

Because of his patient's increasingly poor state of health Dr. Bell advised James to, "refrain from intimate contact with Eleanor until the child is born."

At this point, the master of the house returned to London urgently and stayed there for almost the whole of the confinement.

In her dream, Eleanor recalled her sense of loss as another baby daughter, who only survived for a few hours, had to forcibly be taken from her.

James returned home but didn't even try to comfort her.

As soon as the infant was buried he was off on one of his trips again.

The hurt inside her was almost unbearable. Not only had she lost another child but she had also lost the affection, which she now suspected had been pretence anyway, of her husband.

He had stopped making playful conversation with her or bringing her little gifts back from his trips as he used to, and rather than wait for bedtime he would demand sex from Eleanor as soon as he arrived home.

She heard again the dreaded words "upstairs woman, now!"

They were in the big double bed. He didn't speak but was treating her so roughly and disrespectfully that she began to protest.

This didn't stop him. She felt ashamed for them both.

Panic engulfed her as he climbed on top of her and had his way.

When he was satisfied he rolled her onto her side, placed both his feet in the small of her back and forcefully kicked her out of his bed onto the floor.

Moments later he was asleep and snoring contentedly.
She relived in her dream the experience of lying there for the rest of the night, shivering with cold and sobbing hopelessly.
Against all her protestations this pattern of selfish functional sex, followed inevitably by more unsuccessful pregnancies and then separations when she was temporarily no longer any use to him, continued over the years.
Eleanor hated herself for allowing her husband to treat her in this manner, but she had little choice and a desperate feeling of isolation washed over her.
Any personal friends James possessed were in London, his parents had passed on and his two sisters who he wasn't close to anyway, had married and moved to other parts of the country.
The few relatives she herself had, resided in the south.
She had not been encouraged to make any friends up here in the North, and she had noticed that many people, especially the ladies, of similar social standing as they were actually shied away from socialising with them. Reluctantly she guessed why.
The only people she really knew outside of the house were some of the trades-people she dealt with in town.
She was very lonely and thought about the possibility of engaging a suitable companion.
The more and more money James made them both, the more remote and unhealthy in all ways he seemed to become.
In this dream, as in real life also, Eleanor felt alone and imprisoned, and she prayed for a means of escape.
She was now on an open road, which snaked ahead as far as she could see, and she was running along it.
Surely now she could be free.
A deep dark pit suddenly opened up in that treacherous road, and now she was falling, falling, falling...
Thankfully before she reached the bottom and what she knew would be certain death, she woke up.

Back in real life, she lay still trying to steady her racing heart, knowing she did not dare to drift back into that dream as it might continue where it had left off and end in disaster.
Although now awake she thought again of the past and once more went over her life so far.
She had, of course, spared the innocent girl she had confided in those more distasteful insights into her married life, which she had just been having nightmares about.
She remembered how sad she had been when at six years of age young Jimmy had been packed off to his boarding school and how desperately she missed him, as he only returned home in the holidays.
Three more babies were conceived, but all were either miscarried or stillborn. Memories of heartbreak consumed her as she recalled each loss.
James had seemed able to just forget about them as if they were nothing to do with him.
One blessing was that when told by their doctor that the couple should not try to have any more children, as the next attempt could prove fatal to his wife, James senior took notice.
He announced that from now on Eleanor should continue to sleep in the separate bedroom that Doctor Bell had insisted on her using during her last pregnancy. She still occupied that bedroom now.
Within this place of sanctuary, she would sit gazing at herself in the dressing table mirror for hours, wondering what she had done to deserve such a tragic life.
The sad eyes in the reflection had looked back at her confirming that her peaches and cream complexion was becoming pallid and that her long fair hair was losing its lustre, and yet in spite of this she was still an agreeable-looking woman.
Agreeable or not she had known for a while that another young woman who lived locally had caught her husband's eye.

She had to admit this came as a relief as she had feared he might at some point decide to forget the doctor's advice concerning intimacy and the thought had frightened her very much.

Meg joined the household under James's pretext of giving her a domestic job, but everyone knew she was really there to keep his bed warm and soon she was carrying his child.

As mistress of the house Eleanor had still gone about her daily rounds with her head held high, but she could always feel the servants eyes on her, regarding her with pity.

'Servants always know everything about those they serve,' she thought.

'I must have failed James as a wife,' she chided herself, 'Maybe my fault lies in losing the children?'

Then, rallying to her own defence, she admitted her belief that if he had not treated her as selfishly as he had done some of those little souls might have survived."

Then she thought fondly of the one miracle, which had resulted from her union with the man she had married, her fine, wonderful and much loved son Jimmy.

With that thought in mind, she stopped turning over the past, and drifted into much-needed dreamless sleep.

Part 10:

James Nicholson and his son Jimmy were on the train, heading home.

This journey could sometimes take up to ten-hours, so that gave him plenty of time to think.

He detested Darlington.

It was full of do-gooders and tedious people who didn't share his interests. Unfortunately he needed to have an address in the town, as Darlington was where the original branch of

Nicholson's Bank, his bank now since his father had died, was situated and where many of his clients resided too.

He'd become resigned to the fact that it looked better if he officially lived there for at least part of the year.

He felt again the pride when years back whilst still a boy his father the founder of the bank, who was also named James, had told him that he had business acumen and started to train him up to one day take over the helm.

Unusually this banking dynasty was not now Quaker, due to his father having been expelled from the society for marrying Maria Alvarez a dazzling Spanish beauty, for love.

Maria was a non-Quaker.

That of course caused some scandal for a while.

Nicholson's survived the upheaval however, and still retained most of its accounts, as it was an exceptionally reliable and successful financial house with premises in London and a convenient branch here in town.

James remembered his father, who everyone agreed was not just a good banker but also a good man, telling him that treating others fairly and following your heart was just as important as religion or business.

His beautiful Spanish Mama who doted on her son and indulged him to excess, had undermined this message by assuring him that whatever made him happiest was the most important thing in life and that he could never do anything wrong in her eyes.

To James's mind hers was the better way, as being part of a wealthy family surely meant he had a right to do as he wished.

Due to having that attitude he had managed to upset some local people socially over the years.

He had known that many questioned openly how his parents, a man so likeable and a woman so beautiful, had managed to produce a son like him with so many off-putting traits. His faults included a cold heart, rudeness, cruelty and a reputation for dallying with tavern girls.

Due to resenting them for sharing his mama's affections, he was so self-centred that he was even known for persecuting his own sisters.

So, not surprisingly in spite of his wealthy connections and impressive business skills, people stopped short at offering their daughter's hands in marriage to him.

He soon realised that if he wanted a wife he would need to look further afield.

He hadn't been in a rush to get married anyway, as there were other things to occupy his time and apart from his dependence on his mother's approval, which he invariably got; emotional involvement had never been his strong point.

He smiled when he thought of how his two younger sisters could hardly wait to find husbands in order to get away from him and rarely ever contacted him even now.

James eventually inherited the family firm along with the family home Chorley Hall when his father passed away.

He knew that the landed gentry, engineers, quarry bosses and mill owners etc., on their books had stayed with the bank partly out of loyalty to his well liked father, and partly due to them having total confidence in his own professional abilities to keep their money safe. At a time when some formerly solid banking dynasties were starting to lose their way as Europe gradually began to overtake Britain's lead in things such as engineering and mining technology, Nicholson's bank had never let them down.

James was determined he would never give them cause to regret their loyalty and confidence in his bank, and they never did as James was a ruthless operator and served them well. There were still many exciting new ventures being launched at that time, which he made it his business to keep up to date with. He was quick to assess the viability or avoid the pitfalls of

most of these schemes, and was able to offer informed advice to investors and entrepreneurs alike.
The head of Nicholson's Bank lay back in his seat on the train savouring the fact that he was famous for either assisting his clients to avoid making costly mistakes or helping them make more money than they could ever have thought was possible at the time.
Although still very young his son Jimmy had inherited this nose for where the money was and fully grasped what the changes, which were occurring all around them could mean. James was pleased about this. He had noted however, that there were cases where hopeful inventors would come to Jimmy with unconventional ideas which needed financial backing, and the young man had been known to spend far too much valuable time trying to move heaven and earth in order to link them up with the right people.
James regarded this as stupid when his son could have made more profit by working on something safer, less challenging and not as time consuming.
He was aware that the young man got a great deal of satisfaction from helping innovative ideas become reality and dreams come true, and was as much if not more concerned about those things as he was about simply making money.
He decided Jimmy had too much of Eleanor and of his own father in him, for his own good and that he would have to try and knock that out of his son soon, but not just yet.
That got him thinking about how he had come to marry the mother of his only surviving child born within wedlock.
His own mama Maria outlived his father by several years and whilst she was there he'd had no need to think of marriage as she took care of all domestic matters for him and he could always pay for the company of the opposite sex when he needed it, which was quite often as it happed.

He recalled it was his mama's passing that caused him for the first time in his life to feel vulnerable. He'd long known that there was little chance of finding a bride both pleasing and wealthy enough for his purposes near to home, as most parents of marriageable daughters were of the opinion that excellent banker as he was, son-in-law material he was not. That was what had prompted him to start looking around in London for a suitable match, and discovering from a solicitor friend about Eleanor.

He decided that in spite of the twenty-year age difference, the young lady was ideal for his purposes.

She was young, innocent, wealthy and attractive. Better still her rather frivolous aunt had made it clear that as long as the suitor had money of his own and wasn't just after hers, she was not over pernickety about which gentleman her niece would marry.

He decided to ask for Eleanor's hand and was accepted.

Once they were man and wife James Nicholson could hardly wait to start a family of his own. The thing he wanted most in the world at that time was a legitimate eldest son to pass his estate on to at the end of his days.

That son was sitting opposite him in the rail carriage right now.

He didn't regret at all the fact that he had lived a double life from the day of his wedding onwards, wearing one face in Darlington where he played at being a respectable banker and family man, and turning into an entirely different person once he was back in his London lair.

All that mattered to him was that he got his own way and up to now he always had.

Part 11:

His mind now turned to Meggie, one of the conquests he had made after he was married.

James didn't usually bother with local girls as in those days he tried to avoid scandal in his own town, but he had been very attracted to her when they were introduced on one of his visits back there.

She was relatively easy to seduce, as when he was younger he could be very charming when he wanted something.

Meggie wasn't beautiful but she was very good in bed and had held his attention for longer than most.

For a while she became his exclusive mistress.

He'd enjoyed her company so much that he had brought her to live in his household where, unusually for a servant girl, he had made sure she had her own room.

She would sneak out to visit him every night when everyone else had retired.

That worked well until she had told him she was carrying his child and that had been the end of that.

She thought that he loved her and begged him to get a divorce and marry her to save her from the wrath of her family, which would follow.

He didn't do as she asked of course, as not only did he not really care about her beyond the temporary physical pleasures she afforded him, but that would also have meant all sorts of financial complications, from which he would be the loser.

He had told her that the best he could do for her was to pay his odd job man Victor Jones, who was single and had no other family in the area, to marry her.

After flying at him and attacking him physically, and abusing him verbally, which in his perverse way he remembered he had quite enjoyed, she eventually agreed to this plan, even though the fellow she would have to wed, although pleasant enough was bordering on being a simpleton.

He'd known she would do as he said as he had guessed she could not face the alternative.

At least she would have a roof over her head, and her family would be none the wiser as to who the real father of her baby was, and more importantly no one would be shamed.

James swiftly arranged this wedding of convenience and took himself off to the big city again.

This time he stayed away for months.

Before leaving he told Eleanor what he had done.

At first she was in turmoil and hadn't wanted to accept Meg and the child she carried.

Then, when she had calmed down, said she would agree to let the girl stay, as she knew he was the one most at fault.

So, just as he had hoped, although it caused her a great deal of pain to allow this arrangement, his wife turned a blind eye.

Meg and Victor, were married, and continued to be part of the Nicholson household.

They served the Nicholson's faithfully for years and knew never to mention the past.

Meg's son had became the odd job man on Victor's premature death a few years back, and Meg Jones, due to her years of satisfactory service was promoted by Eleanor to the job of housekeeper when a vacancy for the post arose.

Any feelings of animosity between the two women had dissipated over the years, and although they never became close, they had a mutual bond, having both been badly used by the same unscrupulous man.

James chuckled to himself as he thought about this.

He also laughed inwardly about the time just after Victor's death, when he had deliberately revealed to young Joseph that he was his bastard. This had caused a lot of trouble between the boy and his mother when he angrily questioned her as to why she herself had never told him that Victor was not his real

father.
Almost permanently in London Nicholson had taken to indulging in all the pleasures of the flesh, drinking and eating too much, and only he knew what else. His depravity knew no bounds.
He was getting old now. He'd never been handsome but now was no longer even passably pleasant to look at. That wasn't just due to the fact that his belly had grown fat and his hair thin, or that he had a florid face and black ringed eyes. Those things are just external but this man had an ugly soul, and it showed.
With his fortune at his disposal, none of this prevented him from becoming intimate with many, many women.
He just about lived for his sexual encounters, which were becoming more and more shameful the older he got, and now he was returning home for a while.
This was a prospect he regarded as being extremely boring.

Part 12:

Jimmy Nicholson, on graduating from the University of London had been forced to reside with his father in the city, in order to, "learn the business."
He diligently stuck in and did just that and in a very short time in spite of his youth, was soon overseeing many of the deals and much of the paperwork concerning the applications and investments dealt with by his family's bank.
He found it satisfying to deal with the mostly Quaker financiers behind many of the transactions he handled on his father's behalf, and they in turn being decent people often preferred to do face to face business with Nicholson junior rather than Nicholson senior as although Nicholson senior had been careful to ensure they had no real proof, some suspected his personal morals may be questionable.

James liked this arrangement as it gave him more time to pursue his other more decadent activities.

Jimmy found the city exciting, but not in the same way that James did, and he steadfastly refused his father's constant invitations to go with him on his now almost nightly cavorting. He didn't take after his own parents physically as his father was a typically heavy-set Nicholson and his mother was fair haired and slender.

He had instead been blessed with his grandmother Maria's Latin good looks. He was a tall handsome young fellow with dark eyes, jet-black hair and a ready smile.

Not surprisingly he was well liked and respected in the circles he worked and socialised in, and had no wish and no need to discover how his father spent his free time.

He missed his mother, but dare not reveal this to anyone for fear of arousing his father's foul temper. They corresponded regularly, as they always had done since he had been old enough to write, but that did not prevent him wondering if she was as content as she always assured him she was in her letters.

Now, for the first time for what seemed like ages, they were going home, and the young man was looking forward to it very much.

Nicholson senior coughed, belched, hiccupped, spluttered and farted almost constantly during the long journey home. James tried to ignore him and catch up with some reports he was reading.

There was a stopping off point at York. The older man who had almost as huge an appetite for eating and drinking, as he had for sex, ordered a large platter of food and washed it down with fine wine, whilst eyeing up the female staff whom he insisted on referring to as, "the serving wenches."

Jimmy felt embarrassed.

Soon they were back on the train, and James Nicholson, lay

back in his seat, closed his eyes and snored loudly all the way to Darlington.

Part 13:

It was late in the evening. The whole Nicholson household awaited the return of their master and his son.
Sarah had helped Mrs Nicholson to dress for the occasion, and was proud of the way her lady looked.
All the while that Sarah was assisting her, Eleanor had continued to urge the girl to leave the house before the two gentlemen returned, and not come back until after they had gone again.
Sarah steadfastly refused, as from what she had gleaned from the confidences they had shared she sensed that her mistress was going to need an ally.
Eleanor reached out and squeezed Sarah's hand in gratitude, and the two of them steeled themselves for what was to come.
They didn't have long to wait as the clatter of hooves on the drive heralded that Mr Nicholson and his son had taken the journey to their house from Darlington station, by coach.
Their luggage was unloaded, the coachman paid, and the two men were home.
Jimmy was first through the front door, and swept his mother into his arms before his father could see him do it, and told her how much he had missed her.
James was still outside directing Joseph as to which items of luggage to carry up to the respective bedrooms.
Everyone, apart from Joe who was busy with the luggage, now lined up to greet the master.
He strode in totally ignoring his wife, and barked, "Now what have we here?"
His eyes swept along the line of servants. They glinted with

amusement when he saw that Mrs. Jones had put a great deal of weight on since he had last seen her, and they lingered too long on Sarah for Eleanor's liking.

Then finally he turned to Mrs. Nicholson and snapped "get some wine and refreshments sent to the drawing room, then join me there."

Having slept quite a lot on the journey James wasn't tired, and he decided to sit by the fire drinking wine and smoking his pipe for a while before retiring.

When it got to midnight, Sarah began to feel concern for her mistress. She worried that she would become overtired, by staying up until this late hour.

She peeped through the door, which was slightly ajar, and could see the two figures silhouetted against the last flames of the dying fire.

She felt angry as she saw her mistress slump forward to doze, only to be woken painfully by her husband pressing the hot smoking bowl of his briar pipe under her chin.

She watched this cruel act repeated several more times until she could stand it no longer and after tapping on the door entered the room and curtsied.

"I wonder if Mrs Nicholson might be ready for bed yet Sir?"

"Get out," snarled James, "she'll go when I'm ready to go myself."

Sarah had no option but to do as he said.

She had been brought up to believe that there was a spark of God in everyone, but at that moment in time after what she had been told by his wife and had witnessed for herself, she was struggling to convince herself this applied to the master of Chorley Hall.

Part 14:

There was now a shadow hanging over the house.
Everyone went fearfully about their daily tasks in fear of upsetting the master and incurring his anger.
Sarah thought that Mr. Nicholson's son seemed to be very nice however, and noticed he was respectful to his mother, and spent a lot of his time with her. When not doing that he liked to be out of doors, exploring and rediscovering the places where he had spent the early years of his life.
After that first night when Sarah had witnessed him torturing his poor wife by the fireside, Nicholson senior, apart from bullying the servants, behaved in quite a restrained manner by his standards.
She guessed that was because his son was usually around.
Then two days before Christmas Jimmy went to visit a childhood friend.
It was freezing cold and Sarah was in the barn searching for the housekeeper's cat which had given birth to kittens in there. She wanted to give it some warm milk, and was just about to do so when James Nicholson found her.
"I've been looking forward to this miss high and mighty," he sneered and grabbed her by the waist. Her shawl slipped from her shoulders and she would have lost her hat had it not been pinned on so firmly. She dropped the bowl of milk she was carrying. They struggled furiously for a few seconds, but he fell on top of her pushing her down into a pile of hay. She tried to scream, but now one of his hands was gagging her cries.
The terrifying old man was lying over her, and she could hardly catch her breath pinned as she was beneath his heavy suffocating bulk. She was unable to struggle free and felt sick at the smell of his foul-smelling breath, as he forced his slobbering lips onto hers and plunged his thickly coated tongue between her teeth. At the same time one of his hands was tearing open

the buttons of her neat little maid's bodice and his other hand was reaching under her skirts.

She prayed for a miracle.

The miracle came in the form of Nicholson's illegitimate son. Joe had seen Sarah enter the barn and then watched the man he knew had wronged his mother go in after her.

He didn't like the look of that, so had come to see if all was well.

It wasn't as he could see.

Without stopping to think of the consequences he grabbed Nicholson by the shoulders and with a supreme effort forced him away from Sarah.

The man let out a bellow of rage and staggered to his feet. He saw that Sarah was now on her feet too, so he swung a heavy blow with his fist in her direction, which connected with her temple, knocking her back down again and she passed out.

Now he turned his attention to the hapless lad.

He picked up a pitchfork and thrust it into his son's flesh.

One prong went right through his body so that the point was sticking out of the other side.

Nicholson pulled it back out and then struck the shocked young man hard on the head with the heavy handle, rendering him unconscious too.

Ever since he had arrived back, James Nicholson had been obsessed with thoughts of sampling Sarah's young body and now his idiot bastard had temporarily prevented him living out his fantasy.

Enraged to the point of madness he now noticed a long length of strong, corded twine, which was coiled up and hanging from a nail.

The sight of it put an extremely cruel idea into his warped mind. He uncoiled it and hurled one end over a wooden beam above his head.

The two ends now hung down on different sides.

Nicholson grabbed the unconscious boy's hands and bound each of his thumbs first separately and then tightly together with one end of the twine. He now concentrated on the other end slipping it through a sturdy iron ring secured to the wall, which was sometimes used for tethering the horses of callers to the house.
He began to haul his victim off the ground where he had fallen.
Although the lad wasn't heavy it still took all the older man's strength to lift him, but he was determined to punish the person who had halted him during the fulfilment of his lust. He leaned back straining and straining with all his might, and eventually succeeded in pulling the limp body clear of the floor of the barn.
Then quickly knotting the cord around the ring left poor wounded Joe hanging there.
The young man revived by the pain, opened his eyes to find himself swinging a few feet in the air with a wound in his side and supported only by his bound and now disjointed thumbs.

Part 15:

Whilst the man she now regarded as a monster was engaged in venting his anger on her saviour, Sarah had regained consciousness. She opened her eyes to see James struggling to tie the cord supporting his son, around the ring.
Realising that the best chance that both of them had was for her to take this opportunity to escape. She got up shakily, and then once she had her balance ran from the barn as fast as she could.
Emerging from the darkened barn into the daylight, she had to swiftly decide which way to go.
There was only one option. That was to run in the direction of town to try to make it to Mrs Thorpe's shop.

Sarah sensed that Nicholson had turned round and seen her leave, and was now running after her.
She didn't look back and just hoped that with youth on her side she could cover the quarter of a mile to her former home where her mother still lived more swiftly than he could.
Hearing him puffing and panting loudly as he chased behind her, only urged her on.
She felt like she was running faster than she had ever thought it possible for a human being to run, as if she was breaking through some sort of invisible barrier.
Suddenly Sarah realised that the snow covered street and the people in it looked different. Their clothes looked wrong. Some of the buildings looked unfamiliar.
Nevertheless, she just kept on going, knowing that although she was far ahead of him, James Nicholson would not give up.
At last, she reached number 24 Blackwellgate, and with a fearful glance behind, went in.
She was shocked to see staff she didn't recognise behind the counter and other people in untypical clothing browsing colourful, exotic gifts displayed around the shop.
There was some strange kind of music playing and a heady aroma hanging in the air.
She was confused, but could not dwell on that now, as she needed to get out of sight.
Sarah could see the door to the basement and hoped that once she was safely down the stairs, she would be relatively safe as there were two ways in and out down there, and she reasoned that if he attempted to gain access by one she could make her getaway by the other.
The only trouble was that there was an assistant standing between her and the way to the place that she had shared with her mother, so she pleaded with the stranger to allow her to pass.
Her plea was heeded and gratefully she descended into familiar

surroundings to discover her mother sitting by the fire, there in their very own rooms.
Just as she was blurting out to Barbara that she was in danger from a monstrous man who was following her, a powerful gust of wind swept through the building.
Sarah and her mother clung together waiting to see what would happen next. They agreed that if Sarah's tormentor descended the stairs, they would try to escape through the back door of the building and along the tunnel, which led into Houndgate, something they dare not try to do yet as for all they knew the man could be waiting for them there.
In frozen silence, they waited and waited, but apart from what they took to be the sound of female voices coming to them from far away, and some sort of commotion happening out on the street, nothing else untoward happened. Gradually they allowed themselves to hope that the danger had passed.
It turned out that there was no need to put their escape plan into use, as James Nicholson never bothered anyone again.

Part 16:

When Nicholson turned from stringing Joseph up by his thumbs and glimpsed the hem of Sarah's skirt as she disappeared out of the door, he saw red.
He forgot that he was already exhausted from the effort of torturing the boy and now got a new lease of anger fuelled energy and began to chase after the girl.
He was panting and sweating heavily as he ran, but such was his fury that he ignored this and covered the ground in leaps and bounds.
It was less than a quarter of a mile or so that he followed her, but she had already outpaced him and was now out of sight. He guessed where she had gone of course, as he knew her former address had been the drapery shop in Blackwellgate, so

he headed straight there.
His rage reached its peak. His blood was up and it rushed to his head, as he imagined what he would do when he found her.
He reached the shop.
His podgy hand pressed down on the brass handle and the door swung open, but just before he could burst in a sharp pain in his chest caused him to fall to the ground.
Moments later he was dead.

Part 17:

Mrs Jones went looking for Sarah and the cats and discovered instead her son hanging in the barn.
She screamed for Polly, and soon the cord was cut. Between them, they lowered Joe down as gently as they could, onto a cushion of hay.
His poor thumbs were damaged and out of their sockets, and the wound from the pitchfork was bleeding. They made him comfortable where he lay and tried to stem the blood.
He managed to tell them who had done this to him and what had happened to Sarah.
Polly had been sent to fetch Dr. Bell, and Mrs Nicholson was informed what had transpired.
The mistress came to the barn to help and was very concerned about the young man. She was even more concerned about Sarah, and was hoping against hope that she had managed to escape from James, but if she had where on earth was he?
She was soon to know as Polly returned from the town with the staggering news that Mr Nicholson was dead.
Doctor Bell had recognised the maid standing transfixed in horror at the scene of the sudden death. He told her to run home and tell Mrs Nicholson that he had sent for the

undertaker and was arranging to have the body moved from the pavement where it had fallen and taken to the funeral parlour to be laid out, and that as soon as that was done he would hurry to the big house to attend to Joseph.

Sarah, who had also finally heard the news from a very agitated Mrs Thorpe, left number 24 by the back door so as to avoid the sight of Nicholson lying dead on the ground.

Before she did so she removed her favourite shoes, the one's her father had made for her, and placed them by the hearth to dry as the snow had wet them through.

Barbara lent her a warm cloak, and some winter boots to wear instead, and she set off for Chorley Hall ahead of the doctor. Sarah wanted to find out how Joe was and to comfort her mistress, who almost collapsed with relief when she saw that her young companion was safe and well.

Incredibly Joe had survived his ordeal.

When the doctor eventually arrived he pronounced that the pitchfork appeared to have missed all the vital organs and that although the thumbs would probably always give him pain, especially in the cold weather, the patient would make a good recovery. He then reset both thumbs and strapped them to Joe's first fingers on each hand for support, saying that with time they would be useable again.

Everyone was stunned by the developments of the day. Master Jimmy arrived home that evening, and when he had taken in the news, he quickly took control of the situation in order to spare his mother further distress. Sarah helped him all she could and he was grateful for the genuinely tender care she took of Eleanor.

Not long after that fateful day, and still numb with shock, the whole household attended James Nicholson's funeral, which took place at St Cuthbert's Church in Darlington market place. Once it was all over, and he was satisfied that his mother, with Sarah's help, was able to cope Master Jimmy returned to

London and continued to add to the family fortune.
Unlike his father, Jimmy returned home frequently to make sure all was well.
Life went on at Chorley Hall, but now there was hope and love where previously there had been dread.

Part 18:

Mrs Sangster had done her homework and returned to share her research with us.
All of us had been eagerly awaiting her visit, and so had my friend Bridie, who was so fascinated by the whole affair that she'd spent quite a lot of time scouring material in the local studies department at Crown Street Library for mentions of our address.
One of her finds was an advert in a copy of The Teesdale Mercury from the 1800's, which announced that a Mrs Thorpe Allen was holding a 'sale of clothing at 24 Blackwellgate, Darlington.'
She also revealed that from the census of 1871 a girl named Sarah was one of the people registered at this address.
We all found those facts fascinating but weren't sure how relevant they were.
Then it was Mrs Sangster's turn.
"I'd like to start by visiting the basement again please Beryl," she said to me.
So we both went down there and re-examined the drawing and the shoes, the two items which had finally convinced me to try and make sense of this mystery.
I didn't feel the slightest bit afraid and told Irene Sangster this.
"You are right to feel that way," she said. "My opinion is that we stumbled into a stressful situation which was taking place on this very spot in the distant past.

This situation I am guessing was for a short while linked to us in the present day by taking place on a significant date or dates, enabling participants from both sides to interact.
I saw those two women and I think you saw them too. Also we both know that previously you had come face to face with the young girl."
She continued, "I am pretty sure that they were not ghosts, but living people from another time."
"They weren't dead they were very much alive in a parallel universe and living through a traumatic situation, which we got the chance to be part of."
I gasped at the thought and was flooded with compassion for them.
"Why were they angry with us then?"
Mrs Sangster answered, "I don't think they were angry, but rather that they were stressed in the extreme and didn't welcome strangers at such a time.
When we returned the second time there was only the older lady present and she was settled and calm and didn't seem to mind us sharing her space."
"This third time I don't think either of them are here at all."
I felt strangely disappointed by that.
My next question was, "Why do you think the picture and the shoes are still here?"
Irene admitted, "I'm not sure, to be honest. Some say that portraits not only contain part of the soul of the person they represent, but also that of the person who created them.
Shoes are also very personal and are symbolic of the individual who wore them."
She paused to think some more, "As both the drawing and the shoes can be seen and touched by us all and not just by you, although they are very old they are also very real and exist in the here and now."

She continued, "My opinion is that these items had great meaning for the person they belonged to. Possibly they have remained in this building ever since. I think you being the one to interact with the girl and also the one to find these things are not just co-incidences. It could be that you are tuned into this place in a way that others are not, and so you alone were able to somehow sense that someone with close connections to it was in trouble. You subconsciously wanted to help. That could have unlocked some invisible barrier, which linked you to that girl's world and conversely her to yours.
I'm not sure what the significance of not discovering the picture and the shoes until some time after the appearance of the girl might be, but I'd love to think that you finding them was the girl's way of saying to you, "I was here and we met across time."
A sort of calling card if you like?"
I did like, in fact I liked that idea a lot.
We went back upstairs to join the others, and I suddenly remembered to ask what our wise new friend thought the icy gust that had blown through our shop and the shadow on the floor had meant.
She paused for a moment, and then laughingly said,
"That was probably just a ghost at the door."

If she was correct then that ghost never made it over our threshold, and I suspect that single fact may have influenced many lives for the good.

THE HOMECOMING

Part 1:

Half way up the one hundred and ninety-nine steps leading to Whitby Abbey and St Mary's Church, Simon Wheeler stopped at his favourite vantage point, to look out to sea and collect his thoughts.
At the top of these steps, in the graveyard adjoining the church, his late wife Grace lay buried under the frozen ground, along with their stillborn son.
He was going there to say goodbye.
The icy wind ruffled his brown curly hair and he raised one hand to smooth it back from his handsome but troubled face. In the other hand he held a spray of winter camellias to place on the shared grave.
The collar of his coat was turned up against the bleak weather but he still shook uncontrollably, as much with emotion as from the cold.
A brown leather satchel hung across his body, which contained all his worldly goods.
His experiences here in Whitby had been a revelation but involved unexpected tragedy.
He was in turmoil.
The year was 1875. It was almost Christmas again but there was no cause for celebration for him, in fact the opposite. It was now over a year since the girl he loved had died and he had been trying to continue on without her in this town where they first met. Being near to her resting place seemed to be a comfort at first, but he finally had to admit to himself that there was nothing here for him now except reminders of what could have been, and those reminders were making him ill.

It was time to go back, for a while at least, to his childhood home.
He thought about his parents in Darlington, and about Sarah, his younger sister whose pretty face so full of life and promise he used to love to sketch.
He couldn't help but smile as he remembered her.
Then the smile turned into a frown as he recalled how he had quarrelled with his father when last they met, and wondered how he would be received when he went back.
Feelings of confusion had caused him to leave home well over two years ago. All he was really sure of back then was that the life his parents had mapped out for him was not his true destiny.
He knew he needed to see what was out there in the wider world and discover what he actually did want and who he really was.
Whitby was not as far enough away as he would have preferred, but he knew there was work on the fishing boats to be had.
So, at least it was different, and it was a start…

Part 2:

Painful as it was to do so, he allowed himself to think back to when he first arrived in his new surroundings. First he had found lodgings with a family who lived a short distance from the harbour, and then been taken on as a crewmember on a trawler.
He did not intend doing this kind of work forever, but it earned him a living whilst he tried to make sense of his self-doubts.
Grace was the eldest daughter of the family he lodged with and the pair of them got on well from the day they met. Soon,

with her parent's full approval they began stepping out together.

He had never met anyone quite like her.

Just being in her company somehow made him feel as if one day everything really would be all right.

She understood him better than he did himself and he knew beyond a shadow of doubt that he could happily spend his whole life with this incredible person.

They would talk for hours about everything under the sun, and had become true friends as much as true lovers.

It was she who had suggested they should wed and he had agreed without hesitation, because young women as special as Grace don't come along twice in a lifetime.

Whilst strong in character and intellect her Achilles heel was the heart condition she had suffered with since childhood.

She had warned him of that before their whirlwind wedding. He said that it made no difference at all, as he would take care of her no matter what

Simon now blamed himself for failing to do that, and berated himself for letting her talk him into attempting to start a family so quickly.

He was under no illusion that the strain on her heart from trying to have a successful birth and failing, due to complications, had caused her death and consequently that of their baby boy.

Her parents did not hold him responsible at all, which only served to make him feel worse.

They kept telling him that when their Gracie set her mind on something she would not be deterred and that she had wanted to have his child so much that nothing could have stopped her, but he was inconsolable.

He thought about how joyful they were when they discovered she was expecting, and how he had made a special trip to Darlington to let his own family know the good news.

When Simon had blurted out that a grandchild was due, his father just flew into a rage assuming that the baby was conceived out of wedlock.
That was not the case, but Simon was so angry that he never bothered to tell his family the truth.
Instead he just stormed out saying he never intended to return.
He regretted that his sister and Grace never got to meet, as he felt they would have got on very well.
He was also desperately sorry for Grace's parents, and for her younger brothers and sisters too.
The only comfort was that being a strong family they had pulled together to cope with their loss so far and would continue to do so after he left.
Tears rolled down his face as he thought of how kind and perceptive his Grace had been, and how he had hoped they were set to share a long and fulfilling life together. Their relationship had promised to be a rare and strong meeting of minds as well as bodies and they had so many great plans.
He knew that whatever happened in the future, he would love her forever.

Part 3:

Now he thought of other things connected to his time here in Whitby.
To make his living Simon had first worked on the boats, and then stumbled upon his true vocation.
He had always wanted to be an artist.
His dream began to become reality when one day he sketched a portrait of his captain.
The man was delighted and showed it to all his friends, and from that time on Simon was much in demand and earning

extra money by doing portraits of not just sea captains but of their families too.

Simon was building up quite a reputation for his drawing skills, but being a forward thinking young man was not content with that.

Much as Simon loved drawing he had his mind set on mastering another method of capturing images, photography. He saved up enough money to buy a camera, a stand for it and other tools of the trade. Thus equipped he now set about learning how to become a professional photographer. He definitely had 'the eye' needed to know what would make a great picture, but success in this field was not just about recognising suitable subjects and stunning compositions, it was also very technical, so there was a lot to discover.

He had been fortunate enough to make friends with Frank Sutcliffe, another aspiring young photographer whom to cut down on costs, suggested they should share a studio and work together.

Frank's Fiancée was the daughter of the local boot maker, and the studio was inside her father's premises. Simon's own father also made shoes and boots, so every time they met up at the boot shop to work it reminded him of home.

The two lads studied and practised their chosen art form together with encouraging results. Image making technology was coming on in leaps and bounds. American companies such as Kodak were leading the way. Simon learnt quickly and was now firmly on the road to becoming an artist in his own right, in the art of photography.

They were doing moderately well in spite of the North East coast not being the wealthiest of areas, so Frank decided to try his luck in the more prosperous south.

Simon wished his friend all the luck in the world, as it was obvious Frank had great technical talent and artistic flair but as it turned out the move South didn't work well for young Sutcliffe and he soon sent word that he planned to return to Whitby hoping to renew their partnership. If Simon had let his friend Sutcliffe persuade him to stay, his destiny may have turned out very differently, but as it was even with this tempting prospect on offer, he had known it was time to leave.

He then remembered how excited Grace had been when he'd insisted that that his first proper photograph ever, had to be of her.
He would keep that treasured image of his wife with him for as long as he lived. She had written a loving inscription on it, which he read often now that she was gone.
That thought brought him back to grim reality.
He questioned again why fate had been so cruel. What lay ahead now that he had lost his beloved he dreaded to think? Chilled to the bone he resumed his climb up to the churchyard. Once there, he placed the flowers on the grave and regretfully bid farewell to Grace and their child.

Part 4:

Simon made the journey back to Darlington by rail.
He had sold everything he could before he left Whitby, even his camera and stand, as they were far too large to easily carry. He would buy something more modern when he got settled.
It had been a long trip and he was tired and apprehensive.
On arrival, he had gone straight to the Blackwellgate shop where he had grown up and had been surprised to discover how much things had changed. The sign over the door now read 'Mrs Thorpe, Draper' and he felt a surge of panic as he wondered what had happened to his family.
He banged loudly on the front door and soon his mother Barbara Wheeler answered his knocking.

In his anxiety he started firing questions at her, "Are you all well? Why is the shop name changed?" Once she had recovered from the shock of seeing him she broke it to him that his father had passed away. He was extremely shaken by this news and he confirmed, as she had feared at the time, that he never received the message she had sent.

She described how much their situation was altered now. She went on to tell him how Sarah had narrowly escaped the lewd and unwelcome attentions of her employer and that the wretched man was now dead.

Simon was horrified at all this, and then broke down and told her of his own tragedy.

His mother comforted him as best she could, until he managed to pull himself together.

He then asked, "Where is Sarah now?"

"At Chorley Hall," Mrs Wheeler told him.

Leaving his satchel with her, he went there immediately.

A tall dark haired fellow of athletic build, who looked to be about his own age, or maybe a little younger, opened the door. Simon had expected his knock to be greeted by a servant and was taken aback. This person with his olive skin and fine features, wearing an open-necked white linen shirt was obviously not that.

Simon introduced himself.

"I'm Simon Wheeler, I'm looking for my sister Sarah".

Jimmy flashed him a welcoming smile saying, "I'm Jimmy Nicholson and I'll be happy to take you to her."

As they walked through the large entrance hall towards the drawing room where he had left Sarah and his mother in order to come and answer the door, Jimmy told Simon, "Your sister is a blessing in this house. She will be so glad to see you."

Brother and sister embraced each other as if they had never been apart.

Part 5:

Sarah took her brother to the kitchen where she prepared him a hot drink and they both sat down at the big table to reveal to one another some details of the devastating experiences they had both suffered since last they met.
As they talked many tears were shed.
Eventually, overcome by weariness Simon put on his greatcoat, and set off back to Mrs Thorpe's drapery shop to rest.
Once again he knocked on the door of number 24 and Barbara came up and let him in. He went first as they descended the stone stairs to her rooms.
As he reached the stairwell he could have sworn that he caught the scent of a very distinctive perfume and thought that he brushed up against something which for a moment or two seemed to envelop him and cause him to catch his breath, but he was so tired that he put it from his mind for now thinking he must have imagined it.
He sat a short while talking by the fire with his mother, and then lay down thankfully to fall asleep on a makeshift bed she had made up for him on her own bedroom floor.
The next day was Christmas Eve.

He woke late to the comforting sound of Barbara pottering around in the kitchen. She brought in water for him to wash with and took his discarded clothes to be laundered.
He had been right to come home and felt angry with himself for letting stubborn pride prevent him from keeping in touch. He couldn't help thinking that if only he had known how ill his father was becoming he would have made allowances for the bad temper displayed by Arthur the last time they met, and been here with him at the end.

Part 6:

It was the twenty third of December 2015.
Whenever anyone in our little shop, Guru, has a birthday we always celebrate by eating strawberry tarts with fresh cream on top, washed down by Champagne. Then the birthday girl or boy is presented with cards and gifts. Today it was my turn.
We'd had to wait until it was almost closing time to enjoy this tradition. Being almost Christmas the shop had been very busy, but it was worth the wait.
My workmates know I'm addicted to a perfume called Karma, and to everyone's amusement it turned out they had each bought me a bottle, so now I had three bottles of it to my name for which I was very grateful.
I sprayed some on liberally, and then downed my last gulp of Champagne.
We began talking about what had happened last year concerning the strange events involving a mysterious girl and a 'ghost' at the door.
After Mrs Sangster the psychic lady we had turned to for help had explained to us what she thought had happened, we hadn't spoken of it too much until now, but we had never forgotten it either.
It was late night shopping in town due to it being Christmas week, which meant staying open until nine in the evening.
We heard the town clock strike nine times and that was our signal to pack up for the day.
I popped downstairs to put the lights off in the basement. The others were calling for me to hurry up, so I went into the stairwell and cast one last quick look around to check that everything was as it should be, before I climbed the stairs.
Suddenly I began to tingle with expectation.

The place was lit only by the glow from the ground floor lights shining through the glass window of the door to the shop above.

Against that dim light I saw two shadowy figures walking down the stairs towards me. As they got nearer I could see them more clearly. Leading the way was a beautiful young man with brown curls, dressed in a winter coat. Following behind was a middle aged Victorian lady all in black and wearing a lace cap on top of her piled up greying hair.

They reached the stairwell and I thought the boy was going to collide with me as I stood transfixed before him, but instead he just seemed to melt right through me and I felt a ripple sweep over my whole body as he did so.

I turned in time to see them both go into the front room, and then disappear into the darkness.

I stood in wonderment.

My heart was pumping as if it would jump from my chest, but I wasn't at all frightened, just excited.

After my previous experience of this nature I had slowly come to understand that I was being allowed a peek back into the past. If that was correct then these people were some sort of hologram for want of a better word, of living beings who were also occupying this spot way back in history, and that a few seconds ago our lives and our time zones had managed to converge.

What a privilege. I could hardly contain my elation. Ever since Mrs Sangster, the medium had put this theory to me, I had been secretly hoping for something to happen again, and unless I was totally drunk from the couple of glasses of Champers I'd enjoyed upstairs, it seemed it just had.

This was turning out to be my best birthday ever and I felt this would not be the last time I was to be afforded a link to the past.

When I surfaced onto the ground floor the Guru gang were waiting near the door for me. I didn't tell anyone about what had just happened, and instead pressed the burglar alarm code in, flicked the rest of the lights off and left the shop. Once outside we locked up and went home.

Part 7:

His second Christmas day without Grace hit Simon hard, as he couldn't help but think of how different it would have been if his wife still lived.
He had to make an effort to be normal however; as both he and his mother had been invited to join the Nicholson's at Chorley Hall for the day so that they could be with Sarah.
Mrs Thorpe's shop was closed for the holidays and she was spending Christmas with her sister in Cockerton, so Barbara had been able to accept on behalf of them both.
She was a Quaker lady and didn't really celebrate Christmas in the way many other people did, but had no objection to joining this gathering at all.
She believed everyone had a right to do as they thought best about such things as long as that did no harm to others, and she did rather relish the thought of a tasty turkey dinner.

When they arrived at the hall Mrs Jones the housekeeper welcomed them inside and took their hats and coats.
It was warm and festive in this lovely house. All the fires were lit and a large decorated Christmas tree stood near the front door, surrounded by carefully wrapped gifts. They were led to the dining room where a long candle lit table was set with silver cutlery and sparkling glassware.
Sarah was in the room already and excitedly ran to greet them.

Jimmy Nicholson also came over to offer Simon and Barbara a glass of mulled wine apiece and then showed them where they should be seated.

Mrs Jones and her son Joseph joined those at the table too and soon the first courses began to arrive.

A toast was drunk to happier times ahead. The food was delicious and the people round the table made good-natured conversation.

Mrs Nicholson made a little speech and assured them all that Martha the cook and Polly and Ada, the two girls doing the serving would get their own Christmas treat later. Everyone cheered.

Although Simon didn't have much of an appetite he was very grateful that he had been asked to come.

The inhabitants of Chorley Hall looked so happy, and he guessed it was the first time they had all been able to relax at Christmas dinner in years.

Simon entered into the spirit of things and shared some brandy and banter with Jimmy as the others entertained themselves by unwrapping gifts and playing games.

Looking cheerful was the least he could do, as he knew that if he had been alone on this day he might not have coped.

Part 8:

Some time ago, now there was no longer any danger of the late Mr Nicholson wandering in the night, Eleanor Nicholson had offered her companion a room of her own on the same floor she herself slept on. Sarah had been delighted. It wasn't that she minded sharing a bed with Polly up on the top floor, but to have her very own bedroom had long been her dream. So, it was hardly surprising that when her mistress learnt of Simon's unsatisfactory sleeping arrangements she told him that she could also make a small bedroom available to him as well.

This lady's generosity knew no bounds where her much loved Sarah and her family were concerned. Barbara Wheeler was not left out either, as she was told that she would be welcome at the house whenever she felt the need to visit her children. Simon accepted this kind offer of a room as sleeping on his mother's floor was not ideal, but after thanking Mrs Nicholson added, "I insist on paying rent."
Eleanor Nicholson wouldn't hear of it.
So, that is how he came to reside at Chorley Hall.

Part 9:

Simon now needed to start earning some money again. He had some savings and had added to that money by selling his huge unwieldy photography equipment before he left Whitby. Now he sent to London for the best camera that he could afford and threw himself into starting, at least the art and business sides of his life, all over again.
Mrs Thorpe agreed to make him a space to advertise his services in her drapery shop window, and rented him part of her back room to use as a small studio.
He began to take commissions. He didn't really enjoy taking photographs of babies and brides, but it brought in a wage.
He still wept each night when he was alone in his own room, but out of respect for the lady who had taken him in, and for the benefit of his own family and his clients too, he managed to act normally during the daytime.
His new friend Jimmy had returned to London as soon as the New Year had been welcomed in, and hadn't been back for weeks as he was trying to work through several tricky deals in the city.

Part 10:

Sarah Wheeler grew more and more beautiful by the day. The older she became the more her wonderful inner character showed in her face.
Her brother was inspired to take photographs of her whenever he could get her to sit still long enough to pose for them. Some things never change he thought with a wry smile as he remembered trying to sketch her when they were both younger.

Sarah had several would be suitors of course, but didn't seem remotely interested in any of them preferring to spend time helping, or reading to, her much loved employer.
She had also begun to write stories of her own.
When she was doing this Sarah seemed to enter another world.
Eleanor didn't mind this at all, as she loved it when her companion would read these highly original tales out loud to her and would often give her valued opinion of them.
As well as enjoying listening and commenting Eleanor also asked permission to send some of Sarah's work off to the head of a publishing house in London, whom she vaguely knew through her late husband's banking connections and the young lady agreed.

Part 11:

Chorley Hall was full of joy.
Master Jimmy was coming home.
Mrs Jones and Polly prepared his room and Mrs Nicholson ordered in his favourite brandy.

Jimmy arrived one evening in June, and entered his Darlington home with a big beaming smile on his unfeasibly good-looking face.
Those Latin looks of his had been causing mayhem in London as well connected young ladies vied for his attention.
He bounded into the house and hugged everyone. He hugged his mother, Sarah, Mrs Jones, and all the rest of the staff, except Joe the odd job lad, of course, whom he firmly shook by the hand.
Simon was out working and so those two young men had to wait until the evening for their re-union.
That night was a night to remember.
They all ate well, the wine and brandy flowed, and the talk was animated. Finally it was time for bed and they all dispersed to their own rooms with smiles on their faces.

This must have been one of the only houses in late 1800's England, where all were so equally valued and everyone realised and appreciated this.

Part 12:

It was Sunday morning and in spite of staying up very late the night before, Simon woke early to go and collect his photographic equipment from his studio in Blackwellgate.
He had an important task to undertake today.

In the warm haze of last night's conviviality Eleanor had suggested that he might consider taking a group photograph of the whole household, all eight of them, exactly as they were now. She said it would be something to look back on in future years.
Everyone had agreed that this was a wonderful idea, and Simon felt honoured to have been commissioned.

He would not charge a fee of course, as this was at last something he could do to show how much he appreciated the way the Nicholson's had made Sarah and himself feel almost part of their family.
The weather was fine, so after breakfast, everyone lined up on the steps outside the front door of Chorley Hall.
It made a wonderful scene with all those assembled dressed for the occasion and looking suitably dignified, with the great house providing the background.
They all knew this was a special thing to do and each of them would be given a print of the photograph to keep as a memento afterwards.
Once the image was captured everyone chattered excitedly for a while about how much they were looking forward to seeing the results and then one by one they drifted off to get on with their normal daily routines.
Simon announced that he would go directly to his studio in Blackwellgate to process this special job.
Jimmy Nicholson asked to go with him in order to see how the magic was done.

Sarah walked with them on their journey as she was bound for the weekly Quaker meeting, which she and her mother always attended.
Barbara Wheeler who was standing waiting for her daughter when they reached The Friend's Meeting House, told her son that Mrs Thorpe was visiting her sister after church, as she usually did on Sundays, and gave him the key to number 24 so that he could let himself in.
Once inside the shop Simon locked the door behind them and Jimmy helped carry everything needed to the partitioned off part of the studio, which was used as a dark room.
They both went inside this cramped space and drew the heavy curtain.

Simon felt himself become aroused as Jimmy's body brushed against him in the confined space and he realised that if the light had been brighter his friend would have seen the colour rush to his face. The next thing he knew Jimmy's mouth was on his and the two of them were kissing passionately.
It was as if there was now no photograph to develop, no outside world, no tomorrow, in fact nothing else at all.
There was only the two of them, locked in this thrilling embrace, which both of them hoped would go on forever and that was all that mattered right now.
Neither of them really knew what to do next, but they just moved instinctively against each other until Jimmy suggested lying on the floor.
They both disrobed as quickly as they could and lay down to let nature take its course.
Naked on that hard floor they became willing lovers.
Jimmy groaned with ecstasy, and once their passion was spent confessed to Simon that he had hardly been able to concentrate on his work for thinking of him since last they met.

Simon knew that finally he was home.

The boys hardly dared to look each other in the eye as they got dressed again, but they knew that this first foray into illegal sex would not be their last.
They realised they should try to act normally and appear to be working on developing the photograph in case Sarah and Barbara, or even Mrs Thorpe, came back early, so they did just that.

Part 13:

The photograph was a huge success, and everyone congratulated Simon on his work.

Jimmy said he would love to learn more about how the developing process worked, and suggested that as he planned to make more trips back home from now on than he had done previously, would Simon be prepared to teach him a little more about his art. "I'd be delighted Jimmy," was the eager reply.

Now once a month, under the pretence of needing to check something in person at the Darlington branch of his bank, Jimmy made the long trip North.

He usually arrived on a Saturday and stayed for two or three days.

The Sunday morning teaching sessions in the temporarily deserted Blackwellgate studio became the high spot of both their lives as it was not just photography they were learning about, but themselves and each other.

The sex they shared, although very loving was muscular as well and they revelled in the strength and perfection of each other's young male bodies.

It was the autumn now, and they knew they needed more than just these snatched few hours alone, lying on dusty floorboards.

They had just been physically together again, and lay side by side on a rug they had thrown down to provide a little more comfort.

"You must come back to London with me," Jimmy said, "I simply can't function properly without you. I love you."

The feeling was mutual as they both ached for each other when apart.

Simon agreed this was the only way forward, as these infrequent snatched Sundays were just not enough.

They knew they were on dangerous ground, as what they were doing was against the law and if the wrong people found out

they were a couple they could be arrested and imprisoned.
Both decided that what they had was worth the risk.
It was agreed that once in London Simon would move into the suite of rooms that Jimmy occupied, but for appearances sake would keep his possessions in one of the two spare bedrooms which were normally used for guests.
Home for both of them was now anywhere the other was, so it didn't matter where they lived as long as they were together.

Part 14:

There were some commissions to fulfil before Simon Wheeler could leave, so Jimmy Nicholson went on ahead.
Simon told his family there were better opportunities for good photographers in London, so he wanted to try his luck there.
He added that Jimmy had kindly offered him accommodation.
Two weeks later with assurances that he would come back to visit regularly, Simon left Darlington as well.
Sarah had looked at him quizzically, as she kissed him goodbye, and he wondered how much she suspected.

Jimmy was waiting for the train from the north to get in, and couldn't hide his elation when it did.
He was going to enjoy showing Simon around the big city.
He was going to enjoy living with him even more.
Now re-united the happiness of both young men knew no bounds.
They soon adapted to each other's ways and were in no doubt at all that this relationship was meant to be.
The London society that Jimmy mixed in took to his new friend immediately and invitations for them both came flooding in. Word had got around that the newcomer to their social circle was a widower, still grieving for the wife he had lost, and that prevented any potentially damaging speculation.

Simon soon set himself up in a studio and when it became known he was an extremely talented photographer, he was never short of work.

It wasn't only a whirl of love, excitement, work and parties. When they were alone they confided in each other their deepest thoughts too.

Simon disclosed how confused his emotions had been until the two of them had managed to meet, and also shared his grief at the loss of his wife and child with this soul mate he had so miraculously found.

Jimmy in turn confessed that he'd hated his time at the expensive but disgusting boarding school, full of bullies and worse, which Nicholson senior had made him attend and how his father's lifestyle had repulsed him to the point that he had prayed every night never to be remotely like him.

Each understood and made better the other's pain.

Jimmy suggested that Grace must have sensed Simon's sexual confusion, and had cared for him enough to accept and try to resolve it. He acknowledged that if fate had not intervened things could have been very different for them all.

They both knew that she was forever in Simon's heart and agreed that was how it should be.

Although he never met her, in a way Jimmy loved her too, for being a true friend to the most important person in his life.

Simon went over to the desk and picked up that treasured first ever photograph he had taken of his wife. He read to Jimmy the words Grace had written on it, "Love exists in many guises. Remember that all that truly matters is love itself"

Epilogue:

We should probably end this story there, but I think you will want to know a little of what happened to them all next.

Jimmy and Simon felt truly blessed to have found one another. They shared lots of fun and success and at last knew what real happiness was.
As often as possible they would return to Darlington to visit loved ones.
What more can I say to add to this perfection?
Except perhaps, that on one of these visits Sarah, who long since had guessed what was going on between her brother and his friend, told them that a time would come when relationships like theirs would be celebrated and fully legal, and would no longer need to be kept secret from the rest of society.
They never quite worked out how she could know this, and she would never tell them.
Sometimes Simon could detect on his sister traces of that unusual perfume he once thought he had encountered in the basement of 24 Blackwellgate, and that always made him wonder...

Sarah, at least for now, had abandoned the idea of marriage and was enjoying writing stories concerning people who could travel through time and foretell the future. Her tales were successfully published under the name of S.S. Wheeler. This kind of thing really captured the Victorian imagination and readers clamoured for more, and more. On the occasions she had to visit London to liaise with her publisher she was often seen out on the arm of Jimmy Nicholson, which the gossips decided was proof that they were a couple.

That rumour disappointed a lot of hopeful young ladies but was very convenient for Sarah, Jimmy and Simon.
Only they knew the real truth.

Eleanor Nicholson watched everyone's progress with interest and approval. She was glad for herself too as her own mental and physical health was greatly improved, partly due to being surrounded by people who respected and valued her, and partly from not having to live in fear of the dastardly person whom circumstances had led her to wed.

By the end of 1876 Barbara Wheeler no longer resided in the basement of 24 Blackwellgate, having moved into Chorley Hall to take over Sarah's duties as companion to Mrs Nicholson. When she was packing up the contents of the basement to move she had been dismayed to realise that the drawing of Sarah sketched by Simon, and the shoes made by the late Arthur Wheeler for their daughter, were nowhere to be seen. Little did she know that both these items had been destined to be found by a friend from the future whom would not only help Sarah in a time of need, but who would also inspire her to write.

Mrs Jones carried on being an excellent housekeeper and felt satisfied that the late James Nicholson had got his just deserts.

Joseph married his childhood sweetheart and they had a baby boy together. He continued to work at the hall as odd job man but at a much-increased wage. He now lived happily with his wife and baby nearby at his in-law's house.

Polly, the parlour maid, got married also, and her younger sister took her place at Chorley Hall.

Martha, to everyone's delight, kept on conjuring up her delicious recipes; as she was a very good cook indeed.

Ada, stayed on at Chorley Hall as scullery maid for many happy years.

In fact, if this were a fairy tale, I would say that they all lived happily ever after. To be honest that wouldn't be far from the truth.

How do I know these things you may ask?
Well, if you must know, my friend Sarah told me.

...to be continued.

[signature]

Beryl.

Bridget Lowery